Henry Wallace

Clover farming

Henry Wallace

Clover farming

ISBN/EAN: 9783337872922

Printed in Europe, USA, Canada, Australia, Japan

Cover: Foto ©Andreas Hilbeck / pixelio.de

More available books at **www.hansebooks.com**

LOVER ...FARMING

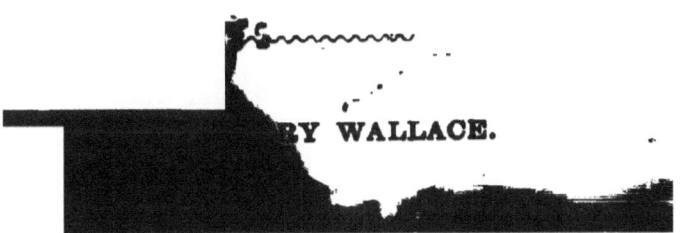

BY WALLACE.

WALLACE' FARM LIBRARY, NO 2.

PUBLISHED BY

WALLACE PUBLISHING CO., DES MOINES, IOWA.

PREFACE.

In the year 1892 I published my first book on the clovers, entitled "Clover Culture." A second edition having been demanded for a year past, I took it up to determine what degree of revision was necessary to meet the present wants of the American farmer. I thought at first that most of it might pass if two or three chapters were prepared by way of leading the farmer, and especially the farmer who had never succeeded to his satisfaction in growing clover, up to the consideration of the main topics discussed. After these had been prepared, I became so dissatisfied with the book that I determined to re-write it almost entirely, with the distinct object in view of making a book about clover that would be interesting from the first page to the last, to the farmer's boy to whom clover is a familiar plant but who has never studied it closely; to the farmer who has not succeeded fully in his efforts to secure a crop; to the successful farmer who had a full appreciation of the merits of that remarkable family of plants; and as well to the townsman in search of information with a view of spending his last days on a well ordered farm.

The present volume has been written from the standpoint of the farmer. At the beginning of each chapter I have asked myself, what is the next thing the farmer, and especially his boy, needs to know on this subject? I have avoided as far as possible all scientific and technical terms, and in stating facts and principles have endeavored to show how they may be applied with profit To what extent I have succeeded in this, the reader is the best judge.

HENRY WALLACE.

DES MOINES, IOWA, 1898.

CHAPTER I.

IF AN observant farmer will take a walk any time during the growing season in the pasture, and note with even a little care the various grasses growing so luxuriantly about him, he can scarcely fail to observe the wide difference between the clovers and the other, or true, grasses. Whatever differences there may be in size, form and structure, he will notice that all other grasses have long, comparatively slender and coarse leaves, clasped firmly around the stalk by a sheath; that they have at intervals solid nodes or joints; and that by means of these they are able, even with a hollow stalk and very little solid substance, to withstand a severe windstorm.

He will notice at the same time that

the leaves of the clover are entirely dif-
erent; that they are very thin—as thin as
fine paper—and arranged, not singly or
alternately on the opposite sides of the
stalk, but in triplets at the end of a small
stem; and that the plants have no nodes
or joints, hence are inclined to lie down
about the time they attain full growth, and
some of them before. Comparing the
grasses with wheat, oats, barley or rye, he
will note that these have the same form
and structure as blue grass, timothy, red
top and orchard grass, and hence are really grasses, the function of which is to
grow seeds instead of forage. A little
reflection will show him that corn of all
varieties, all kinds of canes and sorghums,
are really giant grasses, and all built on
the same general plan as the grasses in
the pasture.

If he will examine the root development of any of the clovers, he will discover that it differs as widely from that of
the other grasses as does the leaf structure
and stalk formation. In the true grasses

he will find a great mass of fibrous roots penetrating, in dry times, to great depths —in the case of blue grass and corn, to a depth of four feet or more—while the clovers send their main roots down straight as far as may be necessary, and the character of the subsoil permits, to reach permanent moisture. They are thus the subsoilers of the pasture field and bring up from the lower depths soil fertility that has been washed down by the rains, and in their decay leave it where it can be reached readily by the roots of other grasses, thus gradually and almost imperceptibly deepening as well as enriching the soil of the farm.

If he will now pull up a plant of any of the varieties of clover and examine the roots closely, he will find on each a number of nodules or protuberances, called tubercles from their similiarity to certain formations in the lungs of consumptive patients. A close examination will show that these are not parasites, or an evidence of disease, nor yet root seeds, as some suppose, but plants separate from the clover, and a fine example of what scientists call "symbiosis," or associated life. Similar tubercles may be found, on examination, on the roots of peas, beans, wisteria, milkweed, locust trees, and some thousands of other trees, shrubs and weeds which belong to the order known to botanists as the "leguminosae," and which always and everywhere increase the fertility of the soil on which they grow. These tubercles are essential to the thrift, if not indeed the life, of all plants, shrubs and trees of this order, and, as we will explain hereafter, are the means by which they alone of all orders and classes of vegetable life are enabled to avail themselves of the nitrogen of the atmosphere. This, as we shall see hereafter, is a matter of the very first importance in agriculture. Suffice it to say now, that this explains (what has been a matter of common observation among farmers for two thousand years) why all crops do well after clover. While all plants that have green coloring matter in their leaves obtain their carbon from the atmosphere, the order known as the leguminosae, or legumes, alone, so far as our present knowledge extends, is the only one that is able to obtain its nitrogen from the same source. While plants of this order obtain their carbon through their leaves, they secure their nitrogen, or that portion of their substance which, when fed to animals, contributes to the formation of flesh, muscle, red meat, from the atmospheric air which circulates around their roots.

Returning from the walk in the pasture and garden, the thoughtful farmer may remember that his father, dead perhaps long years since, often remarked: "We may reasonably expect a good crop of corn this year, because it is planted on clover sod;" or, "We are sure of a good crop of wheat next year because we are drilling it in this fall on clover fallow;" or, "The blue grass will make fat cattle this year because it has plenty of white clover in it." He may have heard his mother, of sainted memory, remark: "When there is good clover hay going into the barn, the cows will give plenty of milk next winter;" or, his father say: "The steers are making great gains because they have clover hay with their corn;" or, "We shall have strong lambs and plenty of them with this bright clover hay for winter feed." He may have heard his grandfather say (with all the pride which old men manifest when talking of their achievements when young men) as he smoked his pipe on a summer evening on the front porch: "This farm was badly run down when I bought it, but I made a good farm out of it with clover. Stick to clover, John, and you will never be a poor man."

If the farmer is a man of some reading as well as observation and experience, he may remember that the improvement in live stock in England took place shortly after English farmers began generally to grow clover, and that they began, in fact, to grow clover before any of the cultivat-

ed, true grasses; and further, that live
stock improvement has kept right on ad-
vancing with the western advance of the
clover area.   If his boy has been to the
academy or high school, and has secured
an English translation of Virgil, which he
has been using on the sly as a "pony" to
help him over the hard places, he may be
able to point out such passages as the following, scattered through the writings of
that wise old book farmer, who wrote some
two thousand years ago:

"At least, where vetches, pulse and tares have stood
    And sta ks of lupines grew, (a stubborn wood)
The ensuing season in return may bear
    The bearded product of the golden year.
For flax and oats will burn the tender field,
    And sleeping poppies harmful harvest yield."
                        —Georgic 1st, Dryden's Trans.

We find Virgil giving directions as to
sowing the legumes in the following:

"Sow beans and cl ver on the rotten soil,
    *   *   *   *   *   *
    Vile vetches would you sow and lentils lean,
    The growth of Egypt, or the kidney bean,
    Begin when the slow wagon r descends,
    Nor cease your sowing till n idsummer ends."
                        - Ib'd.

The old poet had some notions about

clover as food for dairy cows, for he sings:

"If milk be thy design,
Bring clover grass."

If, turning these facts over in his mind, the reader will note carefully the farmers in his neighborhood who grow large crops and to whom farming (and money-making as well) seems to come easy, he will find that they are clover growers, some of them, in fact, known in the neighborhood as "clover cranks," and that clover with them is the beginning and the ending, the Alpha and Omega of their favorite rotation, and also that for some reason their stock of all kinds seems to thrive in a way that is a continual surprise to men who do not grow clover.

Is it not, therefore, worth while to study a plant, or family of plants, that has behind it such a wonderful history; to know not only what it did for farmers twenty centuries ago in ancient Rome, what it has been doing every where since, whereever it has been properly cultivated, but how it does it and how it can be used to the best advantage to grow larger crops on the farm, finer stock in the yards and pastures, and thus fill the home—the best thing about the farm—with peace and comfort?

CHAPTER II.

THE FARMER AND THE CLOVERS.

IT IS no longer a question what the farmer will do with the clovers, but what he will do without them. The vital problem at present is, what will he do to be saved from soil exhaustion—inevitable where the crop is sold in the market off the farm—from soil washing, from drouth as the result of the exhaustion of vegetable mold, or humus, in the soil—inevitable on any farm where grain cultivation is continuous—and from the severe competition of other farmers who know how to use clover. Fertility is the stored energy of the farm, without which the farm is only a place in which fertility may be stored at large expense in the future. The present value of the farm is measured by its available fertility; its future value by its possible fertility. The rest is rock. clay, sand and gravel, of little or no value for agricultural purposes; practically a place on which crops may stand while they use what fertility may be present.

Fertility once lost may be restored by periodical inundation, as in the Nile valley; by the application in large quantities of barnyard manures, as on farms near towns and cities; by the purchase of grain, meals and forage for feeding purposes, as on stock farms in the British Islands; by the purchase of commercial fertilizers, as in the eastern states and in Europe; or by growing the clovers. The last method, in connection with the manure made on his own farm, is the only method at all available for the farmers of the western and middle states, and is a much better method for the farmer in the eastern states than the unintelligent purchase of commercial fertilizers.

There was a time when the farmer could safely ignore the clovers. When the farmers of the eastern and middle states

were clearing out the forests and scratch-
ing with rude implements into a soil enriched by the leaf mold of ages and the
ashes from log heaps and brush piles—
soil, sure to produce thirty, sixty or a
hundred fold—while he was waiting for
the roots and stumps to rot, he did not
then need to concern himself with the
clover question. When the western farmer was breaking out his eighty, or his
quarter, and meanwhile grazing his cattle
on free grass, grown on land owned by the
government or the speculator, who paid
heavy taxes to build schoolhouses, bridges
and public buildings; when the soil was
full of grass roots and his unfenced fields
waved, under any sort of cultivation, with
golden harvests; when the cow could hide
herself in the tall blue stem of the uplands
and the hat of the rider alone was visible
as he galloped through the tall grass on
the bottoms; when weeds vexed not the
soul of the settler, there was no need for
him to trouble himself about the clover
question.

These were the days of the pioneer, when all farmers were equal because equally poor in purse and rich in good feeling and brotherly kindness; all alike soil robbers, scattering with a lavish hand the fertility which nature had been carefully storing for them since the first of all farmers was turned out of Eden, probably because he did not have enough to do to keep him out of mischief.

One generation of soil robbers has generally been enough to waste this heritage to the extent that farming on their methods failed to be profitable. Then came drouths, with no less average rainfall than in the years of abundant crops; for the humus, or vegetable mold, had been destroyed by constant cultivation without manure and without the rotation of grass. Grasshoppers, chinch bugs, blight, plagues without end, then attacked the scanty crops. The mortgage followed, and the soil robber, having reached the end of his tether, and brought up with a short turn, the meaning of which he did not fully understand, was forced to do some thinking and determine whether he and his would persevere in soil robbing or become farmers indeed, and consider, as all good farmers in clover growing countries do, not what they will do WITH clover, but how they are to get along WITHOUT it.

When a magnet is moved slowly through a mixture of iron filings and dirt, it acts as a touchstone, attracting the iron to itself and allowing the dirt to remain. A good strong current of wind will blow out the dirt and leave the iron remaining. The knowledge of clover culture is the touchstone of the farmer when his furrows begin to complain of waning fertility, and separates the men who have the capacity to become true farmers from those who are merely soil robbers, which last are, sooner or later, driven westward by the tempest of financial adversity. The man who will seriously consider the clovers and consider his way to the right use of them, will soon learn the truth (which the soil robber never seems able to learn) that no land, naturally good to begin with, can ever be wholly impoverished by one generation, or any number of generations, of soil robbers. The good Lord, who has ever a watchful eye for the generations of the unborn, will not allow any race of soil robbers to impoverish the land to a degree that will render it impossible for a good farmer to restore its fertility. He has stored the average soil of farm lands, in every place where He intended men to live by farming, with inexhaustible amounts of every element of plant life except three or four compounds—potash, phosphoric acid, nitrogen, and in some places lime. The first two He has locked up in combinations which gives them out in available forms very slowly—grudgingly, so to speak—so that but a small amount comparativeiy, is ever available at any one time for plant growth, and cannot, therefore, be wasted. Nitrogen, without which the ash elements mentioned above cannot be used at all, is, in the form in which the plant uses it, easily washed out of the soil through drainage, natural or artificial, or down into the subsoil, but He has spread over the earth an atmosphere weighing fourteen pounds to the square inch, about four-fifths of which is nitrogen. Not an ounce of this, however, is available except by means of the microbes, or germs, which have their home, or workshop, in the little tubercles on the roots of the clovers and other legumes, whether they be so-called grasses, weeds or trees. It is by these He feeds all plants, and through them all animals, with one of the elements without which life in plant, tree, beast or man is impossible on this planet.

The true farmer who has studied the clovers knows this, and hence does not hesitate to buy a wornout farm at its market value, assuming the mortgage which the soil robber has placed upon it, knowing that a well clovered and well managed farm will in due time lift the mortgage and make the farm a delightful home. This is the history east, west, north and south, at home and abroad, in this land and in all lands.

The true farmer understands that there must be thorough tillage and a seed bed as perfect as possible in order that every atom of available, fertility may be within reach of the root hairs of the plants and not locked up in clods—in order, also, that the moisture may be available that the clovers may have a chance to germinate, throw out their rootlets, enter into associated life as partners with the plants which we call tubercles, and thus draw on the winds of heaven, or more exactly, the portion of the atmosphere that is driven into the soil, for the most valuable and costly element of fertility, and thus thrive and prosper independent of the nitrogen of the soil.

The humus, or vegetable mold, may be worn out by long cultivation on the part of the soil robber, but the true farmer knows that when he comes to plow under the clover roots, with what manure he can command, he can restore it, and his land will no longer pack after heavy rains, or his crops fail in time of drouth when "the heavens are as brass and the earth as iron."

The true farmer knows that if his land be thin and not subsoiled, he can, by a rotation based on clover, gradually subsoil it by the use of clover, the roots of which go down day and night, Sabbath and Saturday, year in and year out, and by their decay admit air into the passages stored with marrow and fatness for all plant life. He knows, moreover, that even if the ash elements, compounds of potash and phosphoric acid, be in small supply, the roots of the clovers can get them when other plants fail; that they have a way of compelling the rocky particles of the soil to give up their stores; and knows that he has in the clover pastures and clover hay a stock feed that will put plenty of bone in his young and growing stock, that will cover the bones with muscles, and, with cheap corn, interlard them with fat. Hence, the man who understands clover is not afraid of ever wasting fertility, or of undertaking the task of restoring it when wasted, by sowing it on land naturally good to begin with.

The soil robber, or the farmer who will not consider the clovers and will not work with them, sells out in due time, or is perhaps sold out; and moves West, seeking other virgin soils, only to find, sooner or later, that there is no further agricultural West, and from a land owner becomes a tenant, from a tenant becomes a laborer, and finally drifts into the city to become a hewer of wood or a drawer of water.

Consider the clovers. The time is fast coming, and in many places has already come, when the clover question determines whether a man is capable of becoming a true farmer with a happy home and family, independent as only the farmer can be, or a soil robber, with calamity sooner or later in store for him and his. Study the clovers.

CHAPTER III.

THERE are families—and families, whether among men, animals or plants. There are families among men, a few—a very few—the name of which is, in itself, a sufficient and favorable introduction of a member to the well-informed stranger; families that have had sufficient sense and family pride to prevent marriages with other families having a low code of morals, and have thus kept themselves clean and pure, living up to their highest ideals. There are other families so uniformly low in their tastes and instincts, so corrupt in their lives and morals, living according to such a low standard, that they would degrade a name, however honorable it may have been once, and make it in time a byword and reproach. In most families there is an intermingling of the good and bad—cross currents of vice and virtue—Baldwins and crabs growing 'on the same family tree; and hence it has long since become a proverb: "There is a black sheep in every flock." "Who, does he take it after?" (pardon the bad grammar; we must quote proverbs correctly) is the question that is asked at once by every close observer when a good family produces a scapegrace, or a low family a noble character.

We may observe the same law at work in our families of live stock, even in those "bred to the purple"—the outcrop of original sin in the shape of a badly formed or colored animal, the result of some unfortunate cross, perhaps many generations since.

We find the same law at work among families of plants. (I am quite well aware, O critical botanist, that the word "family" is not used in the same sense in botany that it bears in stock breeding, but rather in the sense of "species;" but you see I am writing for plain, common people who have never studied botany, and must use words in a popular, rather than a scientific sense.)

There are some families of plants, a few —a very few—that have no positively bad members, although all of them seem to have some far out relations that are of but little account; and were the better members human beings, they would, perhaps, not care to know them, or acknowledge the rest. There are again other families that are so generally bad that we are greatly surprised if there are any members that prove themselves to be even respectable.

For instance, there is the nightshade family, giving us the deadly poison known as nightshade; the henbane, or hyosciamus—an equally deadly poison, although at times a valuable medicine; the foul-smelling jimson, or Jamestown; tobacco, despised by all who do not use it, and many who do. The family becomes a trifle respectable in the red pepper, beloved of

the Greaser; still more so in the ground
cherry; useful in the tomato and potato
(sweet potatoes do not belong to this
family); really beautiful in the petunia,
and lovely in the white flowered nicotina.

It is far otherwise with the clover fami-
ily. There is no really vicious member in
the whole family. There are some members of which it may be said, there is not
much good about them, as, for example,
some of the wild clovers, the buffalo clover, or the sweet clover, which, however,
is only a poor relation and not strictly a
member of the family. Even in this we
may be doing them wrong, and may in
the future discover virtues now unsuspect-
ed. The members of the clover family
have no vices, though some of them have
faults. (Gentle reader, who of us have
not?)

Our present talk is about the members
of the clover family proper. First, as a
matter of course, we take up the best
known member—the common red. It is
not so imposing in appearance as the

mammoth, does not spread itself around
in such a lordly fashion, nor attempt to
smother out the other grasses that seek
their share of moisture and sunlight in the
same field.   It is willing to associate with
timothy, with mammoth clover, or orchard
grass on terms of equality—a sort of dem-
ocratic plant, willing to be accommodat-
ing, to give and take, neighborly in its
tastes, habits and instincts.   Like a good
many of the best men I have ever known,
it is not quite selfish enough for its own
good, and allows blue grass and white clover, those monopolists of the pasture,
(corporation monopolists at that, because
perennial—with perpetual succession—
while red clover is a biennial and expires
by limitation) to plant themselves near it
and finally surround it and strangle it to
death, or at least smother out its posterity.

When the farmer wishes, while resting
his land from grain crops, to fill it up with
the sort of fertility—nitrogenous—for
which all other grains and grasses are
hungry, to grow first-class feed for any-

thing that eats grass or hay, the common red clover is to be preferred above all other members of this royal family. There is no plant that grows out of the ground that will do more, and in so many different ways, for the quarter-section farmer. While furnishing, as do the rest of the family, fertility to the tired land, and of that precise kind which is most valuable in itself—the highest in price if purchased in the shape of commercial fertilizers— the most easily exhausted by leaching— it yields abundance of the kind of pasture and hay that is needed above all others to balance every other sort of grain, grass or forage grown on the farm. While all other crops uniformly do well after clover, all kinds of stock (with the exception, perhaps, of driving horses, and this for obvious reasons) do well on clover hay, and for the same reason. To the soil the clover roots supply the sort of fertility all other plants require and demand as a condition of profitable growth. To the animal the clovers furnish the albuminoids, in which nearly all other grains and grasses are deficient, and thus balances the ration.

The common red is really the only clover that is well adapted to the meadow—on good corn land. On this kind of land, if reasonably rich, the mammoth grows too coarse and the alsike furnishes too little forage. The white clover is not a meadow grass under any circumstances. It is a weed when in the meadow and should, therefore, be treated as any other weed. (Remember that a weed is simply a plant out of place, and the character of the plant cuts no figure, whatever.) Therefore, to the eighty-acre, the quarter-section, or even the half-section farmer, who is a stock grower as well, we say: "Consider the common red clover. It is the best of all the clovers for your ORDINARY purposes."

The common red, however, does not suit the purposes of all farmers, and there are times, conditions and circumstances where the mammoth should be preferred on every farm. For instance, there are many farmers who have been soil robbers in the past, and, having repented, are now trying to reform and mend their ways. These men realize that they must have clover to restore fertility to their land, but do not see how they are to get along without a cash crop while this restoration is going on. They have no stock to speak of, no cattle barns or hay sheds, few fences and no money available for the purchase of stock (beyond their work horses and a few pigs) or to make improvements necessary for profitable stock growing. Therefore, they do not need either the pasture or the hay that is furnished by a crop of common red clover or clover and timothy. What they need is a crop from the clover field that does not need live stock to convert it into cash. This type of farmer should pin his faith, for the time being, to mammoth clover. If he secures a good stand, one that will smother out the weeds, he can reasonably expect a three-bushel seed crop, worth from $10 to $20 per acre, or about as much as any other crop, the cash expense of which, that is, the amount that he would be required to pay for outside labor if he does his own cutting and exchanges help in hulling time, will be about $3 per acre. By adopting a three-year course he can get over his entire farm with clover once in three years and increase his corn crop from fifteen to twenty-five bushels per acre each year, and his other crops, with the possible exception of oats, in the same proportion.

It is quite possible with mammoth clover to secure a month or six weeks pasture and a superior seed crop by pasturing closely up to June 1st, and in some seasons up to the 15th, and then allowing the seed crop to start. Farmers who have roughish lands at a distance from buildings and do not need the hay, can use the mammoth to advantage on such lands.

There are also times when, on account of the ravages of the clover seed midge, it becomes impossible to grow the common red for seed, and the mammoth then becomes indispensable when a seed crop is desired. We will deal with this midge, in common with other insect enemies of the clover plant hereafter. It is enough at present to say that the common clover seed midge is two-brooded and that the broods are timed to correspond with the two flowering periods of the common red. The spring crop of females is ready to lay eggs when the clover heads first appear and before the bloom is on, and the second crop from the eggs of the first are ready to propagate the vile species when the second crop begins to head out. The mammoth, being from two to three weeks later, comes in between the two blooming periods and hence escapes the ravages of this enemy of the clover plant.

While, therefore, for the average farmer the common red is the favorite member of the clover family, the mammoth has claims that entitle it to great respect, and, at times and under certain circumstances, to special consideration.

The modest member of the family is the little white clover, or, as it is sometimes called, the white Dutch. Like other modest folks, it is often underestimated and frequently misunderstood. It is of all others THE clover for the permanent pasture—the intimate friend, the sworn companion and faithful ally of the blue grass. It accepts a hard lot on clay lands, worn out by the soil robber, that have been turned out to native grass, tenderly binding up this broken-hearted land, but fairly revels in luxuriance on rich bottoms. White clover and blue grass seem to us to have been married with a tie so binding that no district judge can grant a permanent divorce. .

Like other married couples, they have their ups and downs. In certain years and in certain seasons of almost every year, the white clover seems to be the boss, crowding out, choking and smothering the blue grass, and in other years apparently disappearing and leaving the field, only to return when circumstances are favorable. It is a good deal of a monopolist, and when it gets out of the pasture and takes possession of the meadow, it is time for the plow, the disc, the harrow, and other treatment appropriate for weeds. From the standpoint of the beekeeper, it is the sweetest and best of the family. It has, however, its faults. So have you, reader; so have the best of men. It is a monopolist, a bad trait in grass or man. It bloats both cattle and sheep at times. In certain seasons, and especially in July and August, it causes the horses to slabber. Sometimes in the hot days of August it makes the brood sow's mouth water worse than the mouth of an eighteen-year-old boy ever watered at the sight of the smoking viands on the supper table after a hard day's threshing. None of the clovers, even, are perfect. Why should they be? We are not perfect ourselves, and should, therefore, bear with their infirmities.

The most beautiful member of the family is, in our judgment, the alsike. It does not offend us with its rankness or coarseness, as do the red and mammoth. Its perfume is finer and more delicate than that of any other member of the family. Its color rests the eye. It does not want the earth with a fence around it. It accepts a place either on the dry corn land, in the slough or swale, and produces, within reasonable bounds, in proportion to the moisture that is furnished. The experienced cow or ewe prefers its forage to that of any other member of the family. It grows no hairs on its stem to fill the mouth with dust or remind the old brood mare with the heaves that there is another winter's tribulation before her. Like all the rest of the family, it has its shortcomings. It produces scantily in dry, or moderately dry soils, and it furnishes but little aftermath. What else can be expected? How is it possible for any one individual in a family of plants to meet the whole round of agricultural requirements, even in one field?

Another prominent member of the family is the crimson clover. Unlike any of the members before mentioned, it is an annual. Like winter wheat, it is a winter annual, sown in the fall, coming to maturity in June, and then perishing. It is the friend of the truck farmer and orchardist south of latitude forty, but cannot stand the cold of northern winters.

There are dozens of other members of this family, among which we might mention the buffalo clover, specimens of which may be found growing, in the corn belt, in waste places; the big headed clover of the Pacific slope; the southern or what is sometimes called the Carolina clover, all of which, while clever in their way and place, have but little interest to the Northern farmer, because they can do him but little service.

The clover family has a great many cousins, some of them, for example the alfalfa of the plains, the Japan clover of the South, the bur clovers of California, are of the very highest excellence, filling their places as notably as any of the clo-

ver family proper fill theirs. We will have
something to say of some of them hereafter.

There are also a number of far out relations (such as the common sweet clover
of the roadsides, greatly beloved by the
bees and their keepers) of which we can
say nothing bad, all of them, however,
storing the soil with fertility, and thus fitting it for the production of the herb yield-
ing seed and the tree bearing fruit, and
thus contributing, in their modest way, to
the happiness of the human race.

It is a great pleasure to find that there
is a family of plants, the members of
which have no reason to be ashamed of
each other—not even of their far out relations.

CHAPTER IV.

THE SOIL ROBBER'S DREAM.

IT WAS Job Barshear's sixtieth birthday. Job was getting old and he felt it. He had been a hard-working farmer all his days. Through rain and shine, heat and cold, summer and winter, in good times and bad, Job had wrought hard, breaking out land and growing grain to sell for shipment to a distant market. He was born in Indiana, and knew all about clearing land, piling brush, and plowing clearings full of stumps and sound roots. He was reminded of this experience on his sixtieth birthday by a twinge of rheumatism in the shin, once badly bruised by a root, one end of which he had cut off with a sharp hatchet he carried on his plow in those days. Every reader who has plowed a new clearing will sympathize with Job.

He had moved with his young wife, full of hope and courage, to Illinois, and broken out an eighty. His crop of wheat on new breaking failed, and corn fell, just before the civil war, to 8 cents a bushel. He therefore failed to make his payments and the mortgagee took his farm—of course. He sent his wife and baby back to her folks and enlisted. He was a splendid soldier but promotion came not, and he came out as he went in—a high private. He had saved his wages, and once more undertook to improve a farm, this time in eastern Iowa.

While he was getting his farm under cultivation all went well. Crops were good and prices high, but about 1867–1870 the tide turned. He fought bravely on until the panic of 1873, then came a mortgage—a veritable tapeworm to be fed with ever increasing bushels of grain—until in 1880 he sold out, moved to western Iowa, and again undertook to open out a new farm. Here, again, times were good and prices high when he had nothing to sell;

but when his farm was all broken out and in full crop, prices fell; and again came the inevitable mortgage.

Meanwhile, his son and daughter had grown up, and as the natural result of hard work for which there never seemed to be any pay, were determined to leave the farm. On this evening of Job's sixtieth birthday, young Job had said:

"Father, what's the use of farming? It's hard work day after day, summer and winter. It's work all summer for nothing to get a job of hauling grain to town all winter for pay; or, work all winter for nothing to get fair wages in the summer. What have you to show for forty years' hard work? Nothing, that I can see, but a mortgaged farm which produces less and less every year."

Poor old Job went to bed with a sad heart, after saying to his son:

"Well, if you must leave the farm, go; I can't help it, though I don't know how I can get along without you. I suppose the farm must go, and that's all there is of it."

And that night Job had a dream. A chorus of voices in the distance, which he recognized as those of young Job and his best girl, and his girl and her best fellow, were singing:

"Home, sweet home;
There's no place like home."

"If home is so sweet, why don't they stay in it, then?" thought Job. "There is not much sweetness that I ever found on a mortgaged farm."

And then the tune changed into

"We don't have to mortgage the farm."

"Much good that does me," said Job. "I had to mortgage mine. It was either that or lose it. I wish they would go away and leave me to my sorrow."

Then came another chorus with new and strange and sweetly musical voices, and a tune that Job had never heard before, singing:

"We'll lift the mortgage off of the farm."

"That's the music for me," thought Job. "I wish they would come nearer."

Nearer the voices came, with music soft

and low, yet clear and confident, until the room was filled with the delightful song, and Job felt the presence of the singers around his bedside. As it ceased the tenor said:

"Job Barshear, we have come, not to mock you with vain hopes, but to put new hope in your sad heart and new strength in your old tired bones. We are "The Clover Quartette." If we are strangers to you, it is because you have not been willing to make our acquaintance. I am known as the Common Red Clover. My big brother, the Mammoth, sings bass; my little white-headed sister is the soprano; and my oldest sister, Alsike, sings alto. Our mission in life is to make farmers happy by lifting the mortgage off the farm and filling the home with joy and peace."

"Why haven't you been here before?" asked Job?

"Because you never invited us. We come to you now only because you are an old man, broken in heart, if not in health, with a family about to be broken up unless you mend your ways and become an honest man."

"Honest man," cried Job, "who calls me dishonest? Haven't I paid every cent I was able to pay and given a mortgage to secure the balance? Did I ever leave a place with a cent unpaid? Haven't I paid debts when I was execution proof, and been called a fool for doing it?"

"Very true," said the speaker. "You have been honest with your fellowmen, paid your debts, your taxes and your church dues; but you have not been honest with your land. You have not been a thief taking things by stealth, but you have been a robber, a soil robber, a professional soil robber all your days. You have robbed every farm you ever owned until it kicked you out; and if you don't repent and be honest with this one, it, too, will kick you out and you will die a pauper."

"But isn't this land mine, subject to the mortgage, and can't I do as I please with it?"

"So is your wife yours, and you know you can't impose on her. ('That's so,' thought Job.) Your son and daughter are yours, but you can't wrong them without getting whipped for it. Your body is yours, but you can't do as you please with it without being punished. You have been robbing this farm every year by selling everything off and putting nothing back. It has been corn, oats, wheat, flax, or corn, wheat, flax, oats every year until every furrow complains of Job Barshear's dishonesty."

"Well, what are you folks going to do about it? Sing some more, I reckon."

"Nothing—not even sing—unless you ask us to work for you and with you. And mind this, Job Barshear, not then. unless at the same time you promise to work with us honestly,"

"What can you folks do except sing and disturb honest people when they are asleep?"

"Do! Why look here, Job, I can give you the nicest fall pasture you ever saw on a wheat field, and next year a two-ton crop of clover hay that will make every cow in the yard happy, and a crop of seed besides, if the season is right; and the year after an extra twenty bushels of corn per acre. You have been saying that you can't grow hogs like your neighbors, because you have no pasture. I can furnish you the pasture. If you have no cattle yet, my brother here can furnish you a seed crop that will help you buy cows and sell milk to the creamery; and then my time will come to work for you. My sister, the alto, can drive the coarse grass out of your sloughs, and my little white-headed sister can fill up the blue grass pastures and fill your hives with honey."

"That means," said Job, "that I must quit this exclusive grain growing and go to farming with stock, grass and grain."

"That is what it means."

"And that I will have to learn a new business and subscribe for farm papers."

"Yes, Job; it means that you must work less and think more; that you must encourage your son and daughter to think, and not work them to death. That is precisely what it does mean; and if you don't do that very thing, and do it soon, you will be a lone hand on a wornout, mortgaged farm that won't be worth much more than enough to bury you when you die, years before your time."

And with that Job awoke, and behold, it was a dream.

When he told his dream the next morning to the family at the breakfast table, young Job said:

"It is a dream full of meaning, and if you will give me a living chance, I will make it a reality."

And he did.

CHAPTER V.

THE CLOVER BABIES.

WHEN a babe is expected in the home, everything possible is made ready for it in advance. The little mother has been preparing with her own hands the wardrobe of materials soft and warm, and with every purchase of material and stitch of preparation there is a thrill of love for the unborn. The father shows an unwonted tenderness, friends are unusually kind, and even jealousies and enmities are stifled, or at least suppressed, in view of the unfolding of the mystery of a new human life fresh from the hand of God. Nature, too, has has been preparing in the breast of the mother the nourishment essential to the new being, and co-operating with human love and neighborly sympathy in giving the child the start essential to the fitting development of a new human being.

The little clover plants are clover babies, and if they are not to perish at the very beginning, if they are to grow to the profit of the farmer, he must prepare both their cradle and their food. If the proper cradle has not been prepared by tillage, and the proper food be not within easy reach, there can not, under any circumstances, be a profitable clover crop.

Vegetable life is such a common thing to the farmer that he seldom stops to consider, what to him is one of the most important of all questions: "How plants grow." It may be well for us, therefore, before attempting to secure a perfect stand so essential to a profitable crop, to think at least a little about how plants grow in general, and in particular how the little clovers get their first start in life. In plant life every original plant starts from the seed, corresponding to the egg in the animal. We say "original;" for while we may propagate some plants by

cuttings, the new plants are but branches
of the old, and not really original or new.
The perfect seed and the perfect egg are
alike the results of fertilization.   It is
not necessary for us, in dealing with the
subject in hand, to go back further than
the seed. ·

The seed consists of a germ, which is
the plant in embryo, and a quantity of
food stored up around it to support it
during that critical period when it is taking root in the soil and establishing con- ·
nection with the atmosphere and sunlight
through its leaves.   Let us examine, for
greater convenience on account of its size,
a grain of corn.   You can easily, with
your penknife, take out the germ, or chit.
This is the future corn plant in embryo.
You perhaps think that the rest of the
grain was made to feed hogs, or cattle, or
man.   You are mistaken.   It was made to
support the chit, or germ, and make a
corn plant out of it if it should ever have
a chance to grow.   The eye of the bean
and potato are similar examples.   If the

germ of the corn, which is really the future plant, is killed by frost and moisture combined, there can be no corn plant developed from that grain.

If seeds are kept perfectly dry, the germs will live a long time; in some plants longer than in others. It is said that peas taken from a mummy, dead three thousand years, grew when planted. Whenever the conditions of growth are furnished, the plant will attempt to grow whether we want it to or not. The first condition is moisture. When a seed is furnished sufficient moisture it at once gets ready to grow, and does grow if two other conditions are furnished, namely, sufficient heat and a little air. It must have all these; not one or two, but all three. You may put clover seed in a manure pile three or four inches deep and tramp it down solid with cattle, or in any other way compact the manure firmly around it, and it will lie there for years, but it will neither grow nor lose its vitality. It is waiting. It has the moisture, it has the heat during the long summer, but it is waiting for air. It will not make another move toward growth until it gets air, or more properly speaking, the oxygen of the air. You may take the same kind of seed, place it in a pile on the barn floor where it has all the heat and air there is, but if ordinarily dry it will not attempt to grow. You may give it air and moisture in the winter, but it will not grow or attempt to grow. It is waiting for the the heat as well. The clover cradle, or in other words, the seed bed, must provide for moisture in the soil, air in the soil, heat in the soil—all three at the same time.

These having all been provided, let us see how the clover baby gets itself born. The first thing it does is to absorb moisture—to take a good long drink. Some seeds require more water, others less, to fit them for growth. Clover requires a great deal because it has a hard shell, and some seeds of it have a shell so much harder than others that they are not able to soak up enough moisture the first sea-

son, but wait until the second year before
growing. In this they resemble somewhat the osage and honey locust seeds
which require to be soaked in warm water
before they are planted if they are expected to grow the first year. Some weed
seeds do not seem to grow until the hull
is accidentally scratched or broken so as
to allow them to take up sufficient moisture.

The water, of which the seed is now full,
proceeds to dissolve the starch in the
grain, and thus enables this reserve food
to move, as required, toward the germ.
This reserve is of no use whatever to the
germ unless it can reach it and be taken
up by it, and it might as well be a mile
away as the twentieth part of an inch. It
can reach the germ only by being dissolved in water and flowing to it, and water is the only form in which the germ can
appropriate plant food. Plants can take
no solid food, whatever. They live entirely, so far as their life is from the soil,
on their drink.

That, however, is not all. The food stored up by nature for the use of the clover baby is largely in the form of starch. The young plant cannot use it in that form, but first converts it into grape sugar, or glucose. To do this, it is necessary to have access to the oxygen of the air. Chemically, starch, the main ingredient, differs from glucose only in this, that the latter has one-fifth more oxygen and one-fifth more water than the starch. Heat is developed at the same time, as usual, by oxidation. This process can be understood better on a larger scale, as seen in the heating of grain in the bin or crib. If grain of any kind is not thoroughly dry and is placed in a pile where there is sufficient moisture and air, the process of heating begins at once, and if not arrested by scattering it about to expel the moisture, it will in time kill the germ. In this case the germ dies because, after starting to grow, the moisture so necessary to its growth is driven out of the pile by the heat developed in the process of oxidation.

We can readily see the starch converted into sugar by watching the maltster at his work. He simply provides the barley, with which he makes the malt, with heat, air and moisture, and waits for it to sprout, or attempt to grow. At the proper stage he arrests the process, and the starch of the barley is found to have been converted into glucose or grape sugar. He uses, in the manufacture of beer, the sugar that nature has made from the starch for the purpose of feeding the germ.

What happens next? Quickening having begun, the seeds swelled, as we say, the food for the infant plant having been prepared by converting the dry substance of the seeds into fluids, which serve the same purpose for the plant as its mother's milk for the little babe, the germ throws out first a root which strikes down into the soil—never up toward the air—and soon after a shoot, which botanists term a "plumule," to be developed into a stalk, which strikes out at once for the air and sunlight, and never under any circumstances strikes down into the soil. No difference how you may turn the seed, even if, as in the case of the clover, squash, and many other plants, the part that goes upward is the body of the seed itself, it never strikes down. but laboriously and apparently with great effort, turns itself so as to reach upward. Have plants instincts like animals or babies? Have they a sort of intelligence? We sometimes think so.

This clover baby is all its life to be a plant that lives in two worlds—feeds in two different pastures, drawing part of its nutriment from the air above and part from the soil below. It catches on to the soil a little the first, but loses no time in getting established in the air pasture as well. From the soil it draws moisture, ash, some of its nitrogen, and carbon, but it obtains the great bulk of its dry matter from the air.

Dry reading, you say? Yes, for the man who does not think and is not interested in the wonderful processes constantly going on around him. But what has all this to do with getting those clover babies started? Everything, my friend; and the main reason why you have failed in the past in getting a stand of clover, if such be the burden of your song, is because you have not known, or would not know, these simple things I have been trying to tell you.

Remember what I have said about the three essentials to the growth of plants—moisture, heat, and air—not one or two, but all three and at the same time. Any one can get a stand of clover in any year if nature will supply these three conditions; if she will keep the soil wet enough and not too wet, long enough for the clover to get the first root down far enough to be sure of water enough. That is all that is needed. The season furnishes the heat, and there is always air enough unless shut out by very deep covering. Under these conditions any one can secure a stand of clover. These, however, are not

the conditions usually furnished on the
farm.

Clover is often sown in the spring of
the year on winter wheat or rye.   If the
soil has a good deal of clay and is full of
water, and there is much freezing and
thawing, the seed absorbs sufficient moisture and secures sufficient covering; and
when the spring furnishes the heat, it
grows and thrives.   If, on the other hand,
the soil is alluvial, or the light drift soils
of a new prairie country, in the freezing
and thawing much of the seed may fail of
cover, and if there is not abundance of
moisture it may refuse to grow; or if it
starts it may perish for lack of moisture,
and the farmer will then complain of bad
luck in securing a stand.   There is no bad
luck about it.   It is simply bad management.   The seed did not have enough
moisture.   It was the farmer's place to
see that it had.   If he had noticed that
his soil was dry in March, and that therefore, no matter what the changes in temperature, there could not be much expan-

sion and contraction, he should have wait-
ed until his ground was fit to harrow, then
sown his seed and covered it deep enough
to get moisture. THE CLOVER SEED MUST
HAVE MOISTURE AND A GREAT DEAL OF IT.
He expected nature to work a miracle for
him and she refused. That is all.

"My father back east sowed it that way
and never failed," says the so-called practical farmer. But your father had clay
land and March was usually a wet month.
Clay soil holds water better than lighter
soils, and especially those of the Missouri
Valley. This clay soil filled with moisture
expands and contracts. Many of the
prairie soils have but little expansion and
contraction during changes from heat to
cold, or vice versa, and sandy lands
scarcely any. Your father was wise; you
are unwise. Remember, you must furnish the clover seed with abundant moisture or it will not grow. If there is not
enough moisture on the surface (which
there is only in certain years) you must
COVER it. It is YOUR business to know

when it has sufficient moisture.   If you do not, you cannot expect to grow clover. You must not guess at it, or CALCULATE: you must KNOW.

Clover seed is often sown with spring grain on the surface after the harrow, and with no covering ·except the subsequent settling of the soil.   If the soil is quite moist, light showers follow for a few days, and no crust is formed, it will absorb sufficient moisture to grow.   This again happens only in certain seasons, and when it does not, clover either fails or there is a partial stand almost as bad as none. Again it is charged to luck, and again there is no one to blame but the farmer himself.

"I was afraid of getting the seed too deep," says the farmer who takes some cheap agricultural paper edited with the scissors and paste pot, "and my paper says that clover seed will not grow if covered more than a quarter of an inch deep."

Nonsense! It is not a question of depth but of moisture.   If the first quarter of an inch will not furnish the moisture needed, then he must get it down deep enough to reach sufficient moisture. Clover will grow on a light, loose soil in a dry season even if it be three inches deep. How much deeper a covering it will stand, we do not know; but in ordinary lands and seasons clover covered plow deep, say four or five inches, will not grow. The baby clover can be born with a quarter of an inch covering, or with none at all, if it has the moisture to dissolve the food which nature has stored up for the support of the germ during the critical period of transformation from the seed to the perfect plant. In climates like Scotland, where this quarter of an inch notion started, there is usually sufficient moisture at that depth. When the soil is thoroughly saturated in any country several days continuously, clover seed needs no covering at all. The lighter the soil the more covering is required. The drier the season the deeper must be the covering.

"But does not clover seed itself in the

meadow and come up without any covering whatever?   Then why cover it in the
plowed field?"

Certainly it does.   Nature, however,
sows a dozen or more seeds in this way,
and perhaps one grows.   She always sows
ten, possibly a hundred, often a thousand
seeds where she expects but one to survive.   Notice, please, how she reseeds
this clover meadow.   She sows the seed
in the chaff, which at once protects it,
absorbs moisture and retains it for the
future use of the germ.   She sows in the
fall and the seed has all winter to soak
itself up.   Stock of various kinds graze
on the pasture and tramp the seed into
the earth, compressing the soil around it.
The freezing of the seed fits it all the better for absorbing moisture.   It thus gets
sufficient moisture, is soaked up all winter, and when it is warm enough in the
spring it grows, of course.   If you will
sow the seed in the chaff in the fall of the
year on a field of rye and pasture the crop
with calves, pigs, or sheep, you will have
a stand without fail.

The above remarks apply particularly to the red and mammoth clovers. Alsike is usually sown on wet lands where moisture is abundant, and seldom needs covering. The white clover is self-seeded, but where seeded as the red and mammoth are, it must, like them, have sufficient covering to secure moisture.

I have dwelt long on this point, and intentionally, because a large per cent. of the failures in securing a stand of clover are the result of not being acquainted with this one simple fact—that clover will not grow under any conditions unless it has enough moisture to thoroughly saturate the seed and keep it saturated until the starch can be dissolved and converted into sugar, or in other words, transformed by the mysterious chemical processes of nature into plant milk. Where abundant and continuous rains do not furnish this moisture, we must furnish it, and that is the end of it; and the only way practicable is by planting it deep enough in the ground to secure this moisture by absorption.

CHAPTER VI

HOW THE CLOVER BABIES GROW.

IN THE last chapter I endeavored to explain in as plain and simple language as possible, how the young clover plants are born and what must take place in the seed before there can be germination, or the development of life. Life is in the germ but it can be developed only by the combination of moisture, heat and air—all three, and not any one or two of these. To secure moisture and thus transform the starch into sugar and start the life forces going, the seed must be placed a sufficient depth in the soil, whether that be a quarter of an inch or three inches, and the farmer must supply this moisture or have bad luck with his stand of clover. Inasmuch as many farmers secure a stand but fail to hold it, I

will endeavor in this chapter to point out
under what conditions, where the stand is
once secured, it can be held in ordinary
years.

The young plant, as heretofore stated,
feeds in two pastures—the atmosphere
and the soil.   From the atmosphere it obtains carbon only, with which it builds up
the carbohydrates of the plants—the
starch, gum, sugar and cellular tissues.
From the soil it receives, through the medium of the roots, the water and the mineral elements, and from the air in the soil,
by means of the microbes on its roots, the
clovers receive, in addition, the great bulk
of their nitrogen.   The rest of the nitrogen, with some of the carbon, comes, like
the mineral elements, by way of the roots.

The plant receives its carbon from the
atmosphere through innumerable mouths,
or what the botanists call "stomata" (Latin
for mouths) located on the under side of
the leaves, and it is estimated that there
are often as many as a hundred thousand
on the under side of a single leaf, for ex-

ample, of the oak. In dry times the plant
has the power of contracting these mouths
so as to shut off evaporation. The effects
of the contraction may be seen in the curl-
ing up of the leaves of the corn in hot,
dry weather.

The plant, by a chemistry of its own,
dissolves the carbonic acid, which is a
compound of carbon and oxygen, uses
the carbon, in connection with the mineral
and nitrogenous elements, in building up
its structure, and exhales, or throws back,
the oxygen to the air. The animal, it
will be observed, breathes air and uses the
oxygen of it for the purification of the
blood, and exhales, or throws off, carbonic
acid; hence, plants and animals are each
necessary to the health of the other.
Without the plant, the atmosphere in time
would become loaded with poison; without the animal the supply of carbonic acid
would in time be exhausted and plant life
would perish.

The plant feeds in the other pasture in
an entirely different way. There are no

stomata, or mouths, in the roots, never-
the ess the plant receives its food prima-
rily from the soil through the parts of the
root that correspond to the leaves. In
clovers, the tap root corresponds to the
stem, the lateral or branch roots to the
branches, and the root hairs, the extremities of which are often microscopic or
invisible to the naked eye, correspond to
the leaves. The roots, as well as the stalk,
branches, and leaves, are made up of cells,
and the growth of the root is simply its
elongation by the addition of cells to the
end or sides. In some plants, as, for example, quack grass, these cells are made
up of a very hard substance, and form a
kind of cap, which can penetrate even a
hard clod. This and other weeds have
roots which enable them to exist under
almost any conditions. It is entirely different with the cultivation of plants.
These root hairs, which are simply elon-
gated cells, take up the moisture from the
soil by absorption, carry it between the
larger cells into the larger roots, and from

these it passes up through the body of the tree, or stalk, and out through the leaves. It carries in solution the plant food in the soil which the plant uses for its growth and development, and finally, for the perfecting of the grain.

It is a remarkable fact that the cell structure of the root when it comes in contact with the minute particles of soil, is able to take from them the potash, phosphoric acid, sulphur, chlorine, lime, silica, and whatever else is needed by the plant, even when these substances are insoluble in pure water. Some plants have a greater power in this direction than others. For example, the clover root hairs will take potash and phosphoric acid out of soils where the grain rootlets and root hairs, such as of wheat, oats and rye cannot find them; and one of the great benefits of clover is that, once wrung out of the rocky elements of the soil and used in the clover plant, the potash and phosphoric acid, as well as nitrogen, are in such shape to be available in the future for other grains and grasses.   Wheat, on the other hand, will take up a large amount of silica, which the clover either will not take, or refuses, the reason being that the wheat needs it for the support of the stalk and the clover does not.   It is supposed that the plant is able to dissolve this otherwise insoluble matter by means of a certain acid secretion peculiar to its root cells and root hairs.

The reader will see at once that if these baby clovers are to grow, they must be given every chance for the extension of the root system, or the rapid addition of cells to their extremities.   In order that this development may take place, the soil must be thoroughly pulverized; in other words, there must be a fine seed bed prepared.   They cannot develop among hard clods, nor if there are vacant spaces full of air where the clover cells can not be in touch with the minute particles of soil. This, we take it, is the reason why so many stands of clover, seemingly excellent, disappear.   The table for the plants, the pasture, the feeding ground, in other words, the seed bed, has not been properly prepared. Fortunately, the seed bed most appropriate for winter wheat, rye, or any of the spring grains, is the one best adapted to the clover plant. Fall wheat is, in normal seasons, quite a certain crop in wheat sections, provided the ground has been plowed early, harrowed thoroughly, thus forming close connection between the furrow and the subsoil, and compacted together, when dry, so as to give every opportunity for capillary connection, or the pumping up of the water from below. Clover, properly covered, the following spring on a seed bed thus prepared, is, barring drouths and untimely frosts, a reasonably sure stand. When the clovers are sown with spring grain on corn stalk land that has been thoroughly cultivated the year before, a good stand, under conditions otherwise favorable, is reasonably certain, provided a proper seed bed has been prepared for the spring grain and the clovers have had sufficient cover ing.

There is, however, another matter to be considered. If an abundance of moisture is essential to the germination of clover seed, it is likewise quite essential to its development through its entire career, and the main difficulty in holding a stand of clover after it has been secured, is a lack of sufficient water for both the nurse crop and the clovers. This, in fact, I regard as the greatest of all difficulties in clover growing. It requires about five hundred pounds of water to carry in solution the materials needed for a pound of the dry matter of oats (including both stalk and grain), about four hundred pounds for a pound of clover hay, and about the same amount for wheat and barley, all calculated as dry matter which is about twelve per cent. less than when in ordinary condition. The reader will see at once that if a good stand of young clover is to be maintained and a heavy crop of oats grown, there must be a very large supply of water in the soil. When oats is the nurse crop, being the stronger, it will help itself to water first, and this explains why young clover in an oats field seems to content itself with holding its ground and making but little growth before harvest. Unfortunately, the hot sun, following the removal of the shade, will often work sad havoc with the tender plants not yet emerged from babyhood.

This fact emphasizes the importance of the thorough preparation of the seed bed, with the primary object of securing a continuous flow of water from the subsoil through the plant; and explains, also, why, when corn stalks are turned under and oats and clover then sown, the results are not nearly so good as when the clover and oats, or other grains, are sown on the stalks and properly disked or cultivated in. The cultivation of the corn the year before has established perfect connection between the soil and subsoil, while the cultivation in connection with seeding has prepared the mulch of dry dirt which, to a large extent, shuts off surface evaporation and thus enables the plant to utilize the full supply of water. The unusual growth made by spring grains that are sown in drills and cultivated until several inches high, is due to the fact that this surface mulch is continued during a considerable period of growth, thus giving the plant a much larger supply of water than it has under ordinary circumstances.

It may be proper in this connection to say something about the value of nurse crops. It may be stated as a general principle, that nurse crops never, under any circumstances, do the clover plants any good whatever. Clover sown alone in the spring and given the full use of the land, makes several times the growth, up to July, usually made by that sown with nurse crops. There are two objections, however, to dispensing with a nurse crop in sections that have an abundant water supply during March, April, May and June. The first is, that to dispense with a a nurse crop is to dispense with a year's use of the land. This is not strictly true, however, for the reason that had the clo-

vers the full use of the land, they would
produce a much greater amount of forage
than can be grown with any nurse crop
whatever.   The second is, that the nurse
crop keeps down the growth of weeds
which would seriously interfere with the
young clovers and would have to be kept
down some other way.   Clovers being
sown early in the spring, do not afford the
opportunity which the corn crop does to
sprout the weeds and then kill them;
hence, the only resort is the mower, which
should be used to cut down the first crop
and give the clovers a chance to head
them off in the next race.

Whether to sow a nurse crop for the
baby clovers is a question mainly of the
supply of moisture.   I am satisfied that
the clover country could be extended at
least a hundred miles west of the present
western limit, provided, first, a thorough
seed bed were prepared, and second, that
the clovers were allowed the full use of
the soil the first year.   Had I land a hundred miles west of the present clover belt

1 would undertake with a good deal of confidence to grow it, but would first prepare an ideal seed bed by removing the corn stalks and burning them. disking two or three inches deep, then harrow thoroughly, and give the clover the full use of the land. If this failed, having prepared the seed bed, I would drill it in as we do wheat, and then prepare a harrow made of ten-inch wire nails and light frames with which I would harrow the spaces between until the clover became established. Thorough treatment of this kind on a few farms would show the falsity of the statement heard in almost every township in advance of clover culture, from Illinois to western Kansas and Nebraska; "This country will not grow clover."

CHAPTER VII.

THE SECRET OF THE CLOVER MEADOW.

TO CONVERT a field of rank clover with the middle head of each stalk just turning brown and the other two in full bloom, into sweet and perfectly cured clover hay, is one of the most difficult and delicate operations of the farm, and one that requires the farmer to have all his wits about him, in active exercise, with the proper tools ready and in complete order. The problem at first sight seems to be a simple one, namely, to let the leaves pump all the surplus water out of the stalk and leave all the substance in it. That is absolutely all there is in making clover hay. Simple, isn't it? Like a a good many other things, it is easier to tell what is to be done than to do it, and a good deal easier to tell how to do it

than to do it yourself.   It is quite easy to
get all the water out—time will do that—
but to get rid of this surplus water and at
the same time retain all the nutrition of
the clover when in its very best condition,
is quite another and a much more difficult
operation.

In previous chapters I have explained
the continuous circulation of water from
the root hairs through the larger roots
and stalk, or stem, and out into the atmosphere through the leaves; a constant
flow, if we could but see it, in which there
are four hundred pounds of water evaporated for every pound of dry matter re-
tained and used in building up the stalk
and leaves of the clover plant.   Making
clover hay is simply arresting the flow
from the root by severing the stalk with
the mower and allowing the leaves to
pump out, before they die, the great bulk
of the water, or sap, remaining in the stalk
at the time it is cut down.   When the clover plant is at its best, in other words has
the most nutrition in the form most easily

and completely digested, that is, when the bloom is as full as possible, by which time the first of the three heads of the stalk will be turned brown, the plant contains about seventy-five per cent. of its weight in water. When this same clover is sufficiently cured to go into the barn with safety, it contains about twenty per cent. of water, four or five per cent. of which is lost by "going through the sweat" in the mow or barn, so that clover hay, when finally cured, contains from twelve to fifteen per cent. of water. The problem of curing clover, therefore, is to evaporate about fifty-five per cent. of its weight in the form of water as quickly as it can be done. The natural passage of water from the plant is through the pores of the leaves and not through the stem. The nice point in the management is, therefore, to evaporate this water before the leaf structure is destroyed by the heat of the sun. The farmer who knows how to do this has mastered the secret of the clover meadow. We could all make elegant clover hay if we could handle it the way our good wives handle herbs for medicine—by cutting it off, tying in bunches, and hanging in the shade. It would then have all its sweetness and feeding qualities and much of its bloom, and by giving the cow plenty of good water she would make as good returns from it in the winter as she would if she cropped it from the field. The farmer's work in the meadow must be done in the open air, in uncertain weather, on a large scale, and with the minimum of expense. He must depend on the sun and wind to evaporate this surplus water, and the problem is how to arrange the work so as to avoid the damage that comes from rain and dew, and to utilize to the best advantage the sunshine and the wind. Given a ten-acre field only, a good barn, and a tedder in addition to the usual hay-making machinery, and it is not hard at all. He could then wait until the middle head is turning brown and the bloom complete. He could start the mower in the evening and cut down

enough for the next day's operations. A
shower, or a heavy rain, even if it lasted a
a day or two, would not hurt this newly
mown clover, because the structure of the
the leaf has not yet been impaired and the
stalk has not lost its suppleness. Had he
commenced in the morning, and the clover become wilted and rain followed, the
hay would have been damaged to start
with and it would have been impossible to
dry it out the next day without more
damage. In the morning, if the day be
fine, he could start the tedder, using a
rapid walking team, or, if he did not have
a tedder he could turn the swath in the
old-fashioned way. It is astonishing how
rapidly the leaves evaporate the moisture,
especially if there be a breeze from the
north or northwest, as the air is then dry
and hungry for moisture. It is quite different when the wind is from the south or
east, and therefore moisture laden. By
noon he could do one of two things; put
the hay in the barn, or if the conditions
were unfavorable, he could put it in cocks

and cover them with hay caps made out of duck or oil muslin and pinned to the earth at the corners. He could go, on with his cutting and cocking and let it stand for a week or longer; then, when circumstances were favorable, open out the cocks and fill the barn up with first-class clover hay.

This is all right for the Eastern farmer. The Western farmer, however, usually has forty, eighty, or perhaps hundreds of acres of clover to cut. When cured it has often less than one-half of its selling value on the Eastern farm, and must, therefore, be made at the minimum of expense. Besides, he is in a country where strong winds with soaking rains are not uncommon in the very midst of the haying season. Hay in the cock, unless quite green, is then in a very precarious situation because if once thoroughly soaked, it is hopelessly damaged and is scarcely worth the labor that it takes to shake it out and cure it. The Western farmer who has a large amount of hay to cure, cannot afford

to wait, if he wishes the very best quality
of hay attainable, until the middle head of
the stalk has turned brown. He is obliged
to begin, if the condition of the cornfield
will permit, a little too soon; for even then
he will be too late in finishing. In short,
he must begin as soon as possible, push
things as fast as possible, and will, under
any circumstances, have some inferior hay
at the last, because the clover has become
too ripe.

In harvesting these large fields he
should cut as much hay as possible in the
afternoon, and as late in the afternoon as
he can. He should aim to put as little as
possible in cock, not more, as a rule, than
he can cover. He should aim by the use
of the tedder, or some form of hay rake
which would make very small windrows, to
secure as complete a shaking up, or turning of the hay as possible, so as to expose
it as fully as he can to the action of the
sun and wind, and then, as soon as a sample bunch tightly twisted in the hand shows
no moisture on the outside of the stalk, get

it into the barn. Hay can be put in the barn or stack with safety a great deal greener than most farmers suppose, provided it has no moisture except the sap in the stalk. Farmers are often greatly surprised at the difference between the action of the sap, or water in the stalk, and water that falls on the outside, either in the form of rain or dew. The reason is not hard to find. The air is always filled in the summer season with spores, or minute forms of vegetable life, which develope into molds, mildews, and such like. These are brought down and deposited on the clover by rain, and with moisture and summer heat, at once start up the heating, or fermenting process, which speedily ends, if not interrupted, with the destruction of the hay or grass. The sap is entirely free from all this. It carries no spores with it, hence does little damage as compared with dew or rain. It is quite true that hay can be put in the barn entirely too green, and especially if the weather is sultry, the atmosphere muggy, or in short, heavily laden with moisture. Under these circumstances, hay is never so dry as it seems to be, and there is danger of mold; if there be wet bunches through lack of sufficient stirring, there is danger of decay, and at certain seasons and under certain conditions, danger of spontaneous combustion. Under these circumstances it is a wise thing to have a stack of straw handy, and if hay is put in too green, cover the mow, or stack, with six inches of dry straw. This will absorb the surplus moisture, and at least lessen the danger.

The more clover is shaken up, either with a tedder or rake, and the more completely the lower parts of the swath are exposed to the air shortly after cutting, the better. The less it is handled after once dry, or nearly so, the better. The great point is to secure, by free exposure to sun and wind, the evaporation of the sap in the stalk through its natural route, the leaf, before the leaf structure is destroyed. After the leaf structure is destroyed and the stalk still moisture-laden, it is impossible to make good hay. We strongly recommend the use of the tedder. Where the tedder is not used, the side delivery rake, making small windrows, is the next best thing, and where a large acreage is to be handled, one of the most practicable and available implements. Any implement which will, in the process of curing, expose the clover to the free action of the sun and wind, is invaluable to the farmer who has a large acreage of clover to cure and wishes to secure it in the best condition.

Thus far I have spoken of first-class clover hay cut from a heavy crop when one-third of the heads are turned brown. There is however, very little of this kind of hay made in the West. Most farmers prefer to let the clover stand until the heads are nearly all turned brown. It is, they say, much easier to cure. So it is. But it is poor hay at best, and if once wet, especially in sultry, muggy weather, very poor stuff, indeed. The sap has been evaporated through the leaves, it is true, but much that would have been digestible cut in due season, has been converted into cellular tissue, or, in plain English, indigestible woody fiber. Most of the leaves are dead and crumble when handled, and thus the best part of the hay is gone —past redemption. It is simply a question whether the man who has taken the trouble to grow a fine crop of clover will go to a little more expense in the way of suitable machinery, hay sheds, and utilize the gray matter of his brain and get all there is in the crop, or compel his live stock to put up with very poor clover hay to their great lack of thrift and his lack of profit. Whether he will or no, the farmer must do one thing or the other. He cannot have first-class clover hay if he allows a large per cent. of the substance of the plant to pass into woody fiber. It is then valuable merely for "filling" in combination with some condensed feed, as, for instance, corn. A late cut clover crop is a poor crop always. Clover hay thoroughly soaked after being partially dried, has very little value. Clover hay so dry that the leaves rattle and crumble on the hayrack is only a part of a crop and a poor part, at that. The best of it has been lost and the rest is largely indigestible.

I am well aware that these losses can not always be avoided, for the farmer can not control the weather. It is, besides, often a choice between neglecting his corn or his clover, and nine farmers out of ten will neglect the clover, because the longer it stands the easier it is to get it in the mow or stack. We can not always do what we know to be right, or the best thing; nevertheless the laws governing the making of the best clover hay are as immutable as the laws of righteousness, and nature will work for us no miracles. She will go on converting digestible matter into woody fiber—indigestible stuff—whether we are ready to mow or not, and whether the weather be fair or foul. She will not wait to allow us to finish working the corn, or to go to the Fourth of July celebration.

She has provided a way for getting the
sap out of newly cut clover with wonderful rapidity.   If we work with her by using a tedder, or a horse rake that serves
the same purpose, she works for us with a
will and with efficiency.   If not, she continues to work right along and against us.
She has endowed the clover plant with a
wonderful capacity for absorbing moisture from the atmosphere, and if we con-
tinue to haul in clover after dark when it
handles heavy on the fork, we may as well
look out.   We will need dry straw on the
top of that load.   If we allow partially
dried hay to get soaked with rain, millions
of fungi spring into activity in the summer heat and moisture, and nature will
not work a miracle for us because we are
good citizens or good Christians.

"Hear now the conclusion of the whole
matter." Have everything ready for hay-
making when the middle heads are turned
brown. Start the mower in the middle of
the afternoon, the tedder, or some substitute for it the next morning; have the

hay-shed or barn ready; keep everything moving; watch the clouds, and as soon as a load of hay is dry enough, GET IT INTO THE BARN. If the weather is uncertain, go slow. Clover cut too late is better than than clover spoiled in the making. If a shower comes don't be afraid to start the mower any time in the day. Rain does not hurt green clover, neither does tedding or shaking it in any other way. Don't trust the boys or the hired hand to run the clover-making without your supervision. Boss the job yourself, and always with brains. Quick, active work for an hour, guided by a clear head, will often save a nice lot of good clover hay, while the delay of prompt action, even for an hour, sometimes brings with it heavy losses. Keep the idea clearly in mind that you must enable the leaves to evaporate the sap from the stalk before they are entirely dead. Sunburnt clover hay, the leaves black and the stalk green, is about the poorest stuff that can be put into the barn.

CHAPTER VIII.

ALFALFA.

THERE is a large section of the United States in which the clovers heretofore mentioned cannot be grown at a profit, for example, in many sections of the Southern states outside of the carboniferous formation, or made soils carrying carboniferous matter. Here they often fail for lack of the proper mineral elements in the soil. They fail on much of the Pacific slope where the long summer drouths are fatal, and also in much of that vast region stretching between the Missouri river and the mountains, where they may grow one year to perfection and fail for three or four for lack of sufficient moisture, to say nothing of the deserts beyond where, without irrigation only the sparse and native herbage can exist. The clovers have also a northern limit as yet undefined.

Their place is taken in the South by the so-called Japan clover (Lespedeza striata) a cousin of the clovers, suitable only for pasture, but invaluable in restoring fertility to lands worn out by continuous cotton growing—on the Pacific slope by two or three varieties of burr clover, belonging to the same sub-family (Medicago) as the sweet clover of the North, and all having the same remarkable faculty of enriching land by storing it with the nitrogen of the atmosphere.

The most valuable, however, of these clover-like plants is lucerne (Medicago sativa), (taking its name from the city of Lucerne, Switzerland, where it is cultivated largely) or alfalfa, an Arabic word adopted by the Spaniards and which has been accepted by the farmers of the United States.

In its origin it antedates history. It has been traced back to the ancient kingdoms of Media and Persia, and we have

no doubt that when Nebuchednezzar was
testing the value, on Daniel and his com-
panions, of the legumes or "pulse" as food
for young statesmen, alfalfa was growing
luxuriantly on the royal farms on the
banks of the rivers of Babylon. It was
brought to Greece during the Persian war
about 470 B. C., thence to Italy; and it
naturally followed the march of the all-
conquering legions of Rome to France,
Spain and Portugal. The Spaniards
brought it with their armies to the New
World, and it soon became established
along the La Plata and Chili in South
America, whence it was brought to California. Its very great value under irrigation having been recognized, it soon became established on the Pacific coast, in
the mountain valleys, and on the plains.

It will be seen from the above that its
original home is in hot countries where
the soil is susceptible of irrigation. The
growing plant has been accustomed for
thousands of years to being soaked with

water, air warm, every six weeks or two
months between cuttings during the growing season, and to dry, hot weather. It
has, therefore, developed a wonderful
length and thickness of root in proportion
to top, the latter attaining, generally, not
more than two feet in length, or three feet
in exceptionally rich land, the separate
stalks not thicker than those of mammoth
clover, while the root may be of any length
from two to twenty feet, according to the
necessity of supplying itself with water by
reaching permanent moisture, and often
half an inch or more in thickness. It
grows rapidly during the growing season,
after every cutting, the time between the
cuttings being measured by the supply of
water and heat, this determining the length
of the stalk before beginning to bloom,
for when it begins to bloom it ceases to
grow. In order to have as little woody
fiber as possible, it should be cut as soon
as it fairly begins to bloom, except when
a seed crop is desired, and this should be
the last crop of the season, the crude fiber

increasing very rapidly after the blooming period begins, and the second and
third cuttings showing much more of this
comparatively indigestible material than
the first.

It will easily be seen, therefore, that in
undertaking to cultivate alfalfa outside of
the districts where irrigation is practiced,
or sub-irrigation is natural, we are dealing
with a plant differing widely from any
other in common use as forage, and one
that is not likely to adapt itself readily to
new conditions.   A failure to recognize
the wide difference between the habits of
the alfalfa and other clovers, or clover-
like plants used for the same purpose on
the farm, is responsible for much of the
lack of success in attempts to substitute
it for the red or mammoth clovers.   To
begin with, desert soils requiring irrigation (on which alfalfa has been for the
most part grown for a period antedating
history) are generally porous to a great
depth.   They generally have in them all
the elements of clay, and in fact under

Irrigation are liable to develop clay beds, and after some years to require drainage. The alfalfa, therefore, has in these soils every opportunity to send its roots down to any desired depth. Any attempt, therefore, to grow alfalfa on land underlaid with rock, very coarse gravel or hardpan must result in failure. In alfalfa growing a subsoil which the roots can penetrate easily without being diverted or forced to a horizontal course is essential to success. Again, alfalfa has for ages been accustomed to a wet surface only for the brief time necessary for irrigation, and this in countries where there is a high temperature at this period of the year. It is not accustomed to a wet soil, alternately freezing and thawing during the month of March, and hence it is very likely to die out in the spring, even on soils where it has flourished for one or two years.

Again, alfalfa has been used for ages as a meadow plant, or for soiling purposes, and it is not to be expected to adapt itself readily to pastures, at least at the first

Plants frequently, and perhaps always, more or less adapt themselves to the situation when placed in new and strange conditions, and it is possible that in the course of time varieties of alfalfa will be developed which may be suitable for pasturage. There is a very considerable variation often, even now, in the size and color of the leaves, stems and flowers. Some varieties when brought from foreign countries, seem to lose their characteristic differences heretofore developed, when grown on the same soils in the United States; while others, and especially those from Central Asia, seem to retain their peculiarities of habit and growth. It is, therefore probable, we think, that in time we shall have varieties of alfalfa better adapted to the wants of the farmer in sections of the country where irrigation is not possible, and where something is demanded to take the place of clover.

It must not be forgotten, when considering the propriety of growing alfalfa, that it does not adapt itself to the rotation in use on farms in the clover countries. As will be shown presently, it is not very easy to secure a stand without irrigation, direct or indirect, nor should much be expected of it for a year, even when given the full use of the land. When once established, the stand lasts from two to fifty years (probably eight or ten is about the average), hence it should not be used in a rotation at all, or if so, in rotations of eight or ten years in length.

I have mentioned in advance these objections to the use of alfalfa, because they all grow out of the nature and habits of the plant, and it is not wise to be carried away suddenly with enthusiasm for a new plant which has been found to be extremely useful and profitable under widely different conditions.

Nevertheless, alfalfa is destined to occupy a much larger place in the agriculture of the United States than it does at present. The very conditions that make a clover crop uncertain are often favorable to the growth of alfalfa, and it has become a maxim that where clover ends alfalfa begins. The experience of the last few years in different sections of the Middle and Northern states has shown that it can be grown on much heavier lands and with a much more compact subsoil than was supposed possible a few years ago. Wherever in the Missouri Valley and west red and mammoth clover do not succeed after a thorough trial, alfalfa should be tried. Where these succeed it is scarcely necessary to look any further. The man who is not satisfied with a first-class crop of clover, or clover and timothy, must be hard to suit, indeed. Where these fail, not for lack of proper cultivation, but because the soil dries out too deeply in the dry autumns and winters, it may be entirely possible to secure hay from alfalfa equal, if not, indeed, superior, when properly cured, to the best clover. It should be freely conceded that alfalfa hay cured when at its best in the drier climates of western Kansas, Nebraska and Colorado, is superior to the very best clover hay.

The man who fails with clover from lack of proper cultivation, will certainly fail with alfalfa. It tolerates no slipshod methods of cultivation. It must have land rich to begin with. It is accustomed to being well fed—a veritable aristocrat in this respect. The soil should be thoroughly prepared, harrowed repeatedly during the early spring in order to germinate and then destroy the weeds, and the seed sown at a rate of not less than twenty to twenty-five pounds per acre, and well covered. It is not safe to sow until all danger from frost is passed. While under irrigation it can be sown with other crops as the clovers and other grasses are in the region of reliable rainfall, we would advise the beginner to give it the full use of the land, and, as it is not a rapid grower until fairly started, the weeds must be kept down with a mower. No stock of any kind should be allowed to graze on it the first year, and it should be mown as soon as it is well started to bloom, whether it be six inches high, or two feet. In short, if we wish to grow alfalfa successfully, we must adapt the new conditions as far as possible to the established habits and tastes of the plant—a rich soil, a porous subsoil if possible, a top soil holding as little moisture as possible during the period of spring freezing, and then use it as a hay and soil plant rather than a pasture.

It is difficult to speak in too high terms of the quality of alfa fa hay when properly cured. In countries that have sufficient moisture to grow clover successfully, and where there is a probability of showery weather during harvest, the same difficulties will be met with in curing alfalfa that occur in curing clover hay, and the same methods heretofore suggested should be adopted. Alfalfa soaked with rain when partially dried, will lose value in about the same proportion that clover hay does under like conditions. It has the same sort of a thin leaf, exceedingly rich in nutritive matter, but liable to lose its structure through hot suns and hence equally liable to fail to evaporate the sap from the stalk, then crumble and fall to the ground.

Experiments conducted by farmers in the last few years have shown that on alfalfa soils above described, it is a valuable crop almost anywhere in the United States, but its particular value lies in its adaptation to soils which, from lack of moisture, or capacity to retain moisture, fail to grow reliable crops of clover. It is a favorite with some farmers on the loess soils of western Iowa, and after we cross the Missouri and go westward, we find the preference for alfalfa over clover increases in about the same proportion that the possibilities of growing clover decrease. I have great hopes that over a very large extent of country west of the Missouri alfalfa will be found to meet the wants of farmers who, sooner or later, must have some kind of legume to restore the great waste now going on from continuous cultivation of grain for sale to other farmers for feed, or for shipment to a distant market. Where alfalfa cannot be made to succeed after a thorough trial on these lands, some other legume, of which the most promising just now is the soja bean, must be found to restore wasted fertility

CHAPTER IX

THE BARN ON FIRE.

BOUT ten years ago, probably in 1887 or 1888, an Iowa farmer, an acquaintance of mine, was captivated with the theory advanced by cer tain Eastern agricultural papers that clover hay of a very superior quality could be made by putting the crop in the barn quite green—merely wilted, in fact. He was the proud owner of a fine octagonal barn about eighty feet in diameter, and he undertook to test the correctness of the theory without taking into account the difference in structure between a Western barn and barns in which this theory had been tested successfully, namely, where they had very tight floors, ship lapped sides, no windows, doors closing on beveled edges and kept tightly closed after

the hay is put in, with good ventilators in
the roof; in short, wooden silos. He
spent one day hauling in this wilted hay,
dropping it from the fork into the center
of the huge bay in the middle of the barn,
not disturbing it after it fell, thus forming,
as it naturally would, a cone-shaped mass
in the middle of the bay. He noticed
next morning that it had become quite
hot during the night, and concluded to
wait until the crop could be cured in
proper condition, and then filled up the
bay with well cured hay. He told me
that the next winter when he was feeding
out this hay to his herd of cattle, he happened to strike the fork with considerable
force into the top of this cone of wilted
clover and was surprised to see it slip from
his hands and go down with apparently no
resistance almost the full length of the
handle. On examining, he found that the
entire cone was charred to blackness, the
structure of the hay disorganized, and was
still more surprised to find that his cattle
ate it with great relish. This affords a fine

example of combustion of hay WITHOUT flame, and the circumstances forbid any other conclusion than that it was spontaneous.

In the autumn of 1889, a farmer living near Marshalltown, Iowa, built a number of stacks of clover hay in his meadow, one of them from material quite green, the rest after it was well cured. The stack first built was observed to steam in the early mornings for some days, and afterward to sink in at the top near the center. Horses running in the field after the aftermath furnished a full bite, having access to all the stacks, seemed to prefer this stack to all others, and ate in some distance all around. One morning, when the owner happened to be looking in the direction of the stack, it burst into flame at the top and burned to the ground, the rest of the stacks remaining in good condition. This furnishes an example of combustion that was evidently spontaneous WITH flame.

In the last ten days of August and the

first fifteen days of September, about one hundred cases of barn and stack fires were reported from northern Iowa (many of the reports being made to me personally) together with a few in the central and southern portions.   From a mass of correspondence received about that time, when the subject was attracting large attention in Iowa and adjoining states, I give the following sample:

"Enclosed find a sample of clover hay put up in June, on the third day after cutting, in a barn that would hold a hundred tons.   It became so hot that it could not be held in the naked hand, and tons of it are completely spoiled.   Farmers are in a panic here about their hay.   Stacks and barns are taking fire and they do not know what to do.   Fifty tons of hay burned within one-half mile of my own farm last night, from its own heat.   This hay was watched, as it was expected to burn, and there was no question as to its cause. One barn two miles east of here was emptied of its hay day before yesterday, which was already on fire in the inside of the mow and kept down by water till it was hauled out to the field.   After being hauled out, it took fire and burned completely up."

H. R. LEAMING, Wyoming, Iowa.

About the same time the barn of Mr. L. G. Clute, of Manchester, Iowa, took fire in a very mysterious way and burned to the ground. It was insured in the Farmers' Insurance Company, of Cedar Rapids, Iowa. The adjuster made a personal investigation and reported to his company, which report was published in the Cedar Rapids, (Iowa) Gazette, as follows:

The barn was 60x100 feet, the mow being 40x90 feet, and 30 feet deep, containing nearly five hundred tons of hay. Early in haying season green clover had been put in one bent, and ever since it had been heating until at last it took fire by spontaneous combustion. When discovered, there was in three chimney holes, as the neighbors called them, a blue blaze springing out over each, some two or three feet under the roof. The fire was located far beneath at the depth of thirty feet. * * This blue blaze was gas, and the depths beneath were gas wells on a small scale. One hundred and three neighbors collected to fight the fire and worked two days and nights to save the hay. Thirteen out of the one hundred and three succumbed to the effects of the gas and had to stop work, one being so violently ill as a result that he is not likely to recover.

A Chicago journal, of August 28, 1889, contained an article on the subject by Professor Sanborn, formerly director of the Missouri Experiment Station, as follows:

In fact, I never knew before this case, of a barn burning where either lightning, coal oil lanterns, or satisfactory evidence of incendiarism—generally for insurance—was not the easily inciting cause. Hay or fodder that is green enough to ferment will pack closely in a mow by its very weight, and as it heats it settles closer and closer, of course excluding the circulation of air, except it be by a very slow movement. As the hotter part is the center of the mow, it will be seen to be very doubtful whether air, always essential to flame, will be present in amount sufficient to produce flame. I doubt whether spontaneous combustion of hay or corn fodder is possible.

I quote this as an illustration of the skepticism of really scientific men as to the possibility of spontaneous combustion of hay. On reading the article I sent the professor a sample of charred clover hay that I had received a day or two before from Mr. C. H. Seager, of Gilman, Iowa, whose barn had recently been burned, and received the following reply:

All preconceived views of the matter are puerile before facts. The charred material looks much like matter burned in an air insufficient for full combustion. Charring does not imply flame, but rather the contrary. The heating of green food in the mow is due to a ferment, and not to direct oxidation, in the old sense of the word, or in the sense that wood is burned. Will the ferments (low plant life) thus produce self-destruction or carry fermenation forward until it becomes oxidation? Fermentation ceases with lack of moisture, and flame will not occur where it is abundant. I confess I never saw such charred material as you have forwarded to me. While it does not follow that combustion need be the result, I confess to the belief that the circumstances do not warrant the denial of the possibility of it, at least by me, with the evidence before me. I hope that you will obtain the views of the highest biological authority in the country, for the question is an interesting and important one."

While I know of no instance of spontaneous combustion where the hay was pure

timothy or prairie grass, clover is not the
only forage that is liable to take fire in
this mysterious way. In the fall of 1894,
owing to the extreme drouth of that year
and the scarcity of hay, an unusually large
amount of corn in the West was put in
shock and much of it shredded for cattle
feed. Mr. Martin Flynn, of Des Moines,
Iowa, who has a farm of fifteen hundred
acres on the Des Moines, Northern &
Western railway, at Flynn Station, a few
miles out of Des Moines, built a hay
shed eighty feet long, about twenty-five
feet in width, and of the usual height. He
had a field of eighty acres of corn which
he cut for fodder and shredded, and at the
first stored about two-thirds of it in this
barn. He noticed that, when about two-
thirds of it was shredded, the mass was
becoming very hot, and removed the shred-
der to another field of corn which he had
purchased for winter forage. Fearing
spontaneous combustion, he cut trenches
across the shed and laid a continuous row
of tiles in each trench, ditch fashion, in

order to allow the accumulating heat to escape. The mass seemed to cool down after the operation, and thinking all danger passed, he shredded the remaining one-third of this eighty acres and filled up the shed. One afternoon some weeks afterwards, and probably about two months from the time the first fifty acres were shredded, the shed took fire and burned to the ground. He believes that if he had not put the last twenty-six acres of shredded fodder into this shed there would have been no fire.

He had stored a large amount of shredded fodder in his large barn, and on examining it he found it heating, and cut trenches down through it for the purpose of ventilation. In the center it was very dry and some of it charred and black; but near the bottom there was some moisture remaining. No further damage occurred.

In the fall of 1897, Mr. Flynn had a stack of millet hay take fire under the following conditions: When the millet of which it was composed began to cover the ground in the spring, he noticed that some skips had been made by the man who sowed it. He had these strips re-sown, some quite thickly by mistake, and the rest with the usual allowance of seed. A rain came on immediately after sowing and a fine growth was the result. The entire field was mown at the same time and stacked, the millet from the first sowing being quite dry—too dry, in fact—but that from the strips quite green. All was stacked together on Saturday, but not topped out for lack of time. On topping it out on Monday it was observed to be quite hot on the northwestern corner. Afterward it became hot all over, and for this reason was watched very closely. It seemed, however, to cool off in time, but began to settle in at the top and was, therefore, watched the more closely. The land around the stack, as well as the entire field, had been fall plowed in the usual course of farm operations. One morning, a little after daylight, some weeks after it it had been built, it was discovered to break out in flame and burned to the ground.

I have gone into the above minute details, because the scientific mind in the United States seems quite unwilling to admit the possibility of the spontaneous combustion of clover hay or other forage, and in the above examples, occurring over a period of ten years, I present an array of facts, all of them derived from thoroughly reliable sources, which can be accounted for, in my judgment, in but one way, namely, spontaneous combustion. They are but a small portion of facts collected in the last ten years, all pointing to the same conclusion. Mr. J. W. Bopp, of Fayette county, investigated, during the fall of 1889 (in which there were more cases of spontaneous combustion reported than in all the years following) some fifty cases occurring in northeastern Iowa. In all, or at least in nearly all the instances, the hay was put in damp, either from rain or dew, or with wet bunches interspersed, the result of attempting to cure a heavy crop without the use of the tedder. In most of the cases into which we have inquired, the hay was placed on timbers that furnished an opportunity for the moderately free access of air from beneath.

It will be noticed in every case that these mysterious fires did not occur until some weeks after the hay or other forage was stored in the barn or stack, and, where observations were made, until after the heat developed had time to drive the moisture —not merely the surplus, but the fixed moisture—from the mass. I know of no instance in which fire has occurred while vapor could be seen arising from the barn or stack in the morning, nor, indeed, for some considerable time afterwards. When the barn, shed, or stack was suspected, as in many of the cases reported to me, and closely watched, the fire did not occur until the mass had begun to cool down. In one case, not cited above, the farmer discovered certain funnels or craters near the center of the mass from which there was a constant current of what seemed to be gas, similar to that mentioned by the adjuster of the Farmers' Insurance Company in the Clute instance. He lowered an egg into one of these openings and found that the gas consumed the shell and dried out the contents without burning them.

The conclusions we can draw from these facts are the following:

That spontaneous combustion of clover hay, corn fodder and millet is possible.

That it is much more frequent in certain years than in others, and in certain sections than in other sections of the same state.

That it does not occur until all the moisture, whether fixed or excess, has been expelled by the heat, nor until from four to eight weeks after the hay has been stored.

That it is dangerous to put large amounts of very imperfectly cured forage, or forage containing over twenty per cent. of moisture, in a large bay, and that the more compactly the mass settles the more dangerous it becomes.

That when hay containing a surplus of moisture is allowed to drop from the horse fork continually in one place, a danger point is established, and it becomes the more dangerous because on the center line of the bay.

The observant farmer will find, if he watches his hay barn closely when putting in hay a trifle green, much that will confirm the correctness of the conclusions above drawn. For example, if, after putting in a few loads of hay which he knows to have been imperfectly cured, and especially if it has been wet with dew or rain, or brought in late, or on a day when the atmosphere is heavily laden with moisture, he will examine the surface of the mow next morning, it will be found apparently wet, and especially at the points where a large number of forkfuls were dropped in succession. What has happened during the night? Every kind of forage, and especially clover hay, brings with it to the barn unnumbered millions of minute microscopic plants, which it is sufficient for our present purpose to describe under the general name of fungus. These, with moisture, under a summer temperature, at once begin to grow, and with great rapidity, and one of the universal evidences of their growth is the development of a large amount of heat. No matter how dry grain may be put in a stack, under the atmospheric conditions prevailing in humid regions, heating will result; or, as the farmer says, the grain in the stack or mow "goes through the sweat." Given a large amount of this damp hay and time enough for the heat to dry out, not only the surplus but the fixed moisture, usually from ten to fifteen per cent. in grain, and from fifteen to twenty-five in forage, and there is a possibility of combustion, whether accompanied by flame or not. It is said by scientists that the microscopic plants which we call by the general name of fungi, have power to develop a heat of one hundred and forty-five degrees, which then proves fatal to themselves. If this heat is not sufficient to drive out the moisture in the mass, as in the case of silage, whether in the stack or silo, no spontaneous combustion will occur. It is a well known fact that in the climate of England, in wet seasons, hay of all kinds is put up directly from the swath, and even wet with rain, into stacks which are made as solid as possible by running over them a heavy iron roller, and that this forage keeps reasonably well, being, in fact, a form of silage. The immediate cause of spontaneous combustion seems to be by the development of gases which, on account of the compactness of the mass, are not allowed to escape.

I do not care to enter into any scientific discussion of the subject, for two reasons: First, it would make the chapter entirely too long; and second, I have never yet seen any satisfactory explanation of the cause of the development of gases under the conditions mentioned, and it is needless to say that I am not competent to form any explanation of my own. My aim is to point out the real danger and offer suggestions as to how this danger may possibly be avoided.

First, do not build a hay bay over twenty feet high nor over thirty feet wide, and see that every bay of these dimensions is provided with a good ventilator in the roof, and no ventilation in the bottom. I prefer putting clover, or other hay, directly on the ground, dry, of course, for the double purpose of shutting out ventilation from below and of economy in the construction of the building, thus taking the weight of the hay from the timbers. The more perfect the roof ventilation, the greater the opportunity for the escape of the heat and gases that may be developed in the mass.

Second, be careful about storing clover, corn fodder, or millet with a surplus of moisture. They can safely carry about twenty per cent., which is about the average amount when clover-hay is stored in good condition, the leaves and stalk being dry but not brittle; and be especially careful when this moisture is made up,

not of the sap in the plant, but of rain or
dew, or where the atmosphere is saturated
with moisture, as it frequently is at sundown, and sometimes all day during the
haying season.

Third, do not allow the fork to drop its
load in one spot or along the center.   It
is better to have a hand in the mow to
swing it from one side to another as needed, and to store it as it had to be stored
or mowed away before the advent of the
horse fork.

Fourth, let the hay rest on the ground
and not on loose boards or rails, which
provide for a current of air from beneath.
In short, let out the heat and gas if it ac-
cumulates, from above, but shut out the
air from below.

From the above statements and conclusions the farmer must be the best judge as
to what he had better do in case his barn
is in danger from spontaneous combustion.
If it was my own case, I would in the
earlier stages follow the example of Mr.
Flynn, above mentioned; that is, I would

provide in some way a means of escape for the gas. If, however, combustion has already begun without flame, and the opening of the mass would admit air freely, I would prefer, in order to save the barn, to smother it out in some way by excluding the air. If it were in a stack, I would let it alone and make further independent observations as to the mysterious phenomena of spontaneous combustion.

CHAPTER X.

A CROP OF CLOVER SEED.

IN THE production of a paying crop of clover seed, three forces must work together and with a will, nature, man and bumble bees, or more strictly speaking, insects; and if these do not work together, the seed crop will be, to a greater or less extent, a failure. There must be a good stand to begin with, of plants long enough to be handled with the usual implements without waste, and yet not too rank, and ripening evenly at the same time. This presupposes on nature's part a good soil and season, and on man's part even sowing in a well prepared seed bed, and in general good management; but with all these and without the co-operation of insects, not a single grain of clover seed can be formed.

I said all this one day when visiting my friend, Job Barshear, at his farm. He was willing to admit the necessity of the co-operation of nature and man, but he evidently did not believe even a little bit in the necessity for the co-operation of insects. He said to me (if I recollect aright it was about the 10th of July) as he looked out on young Job's first ten-acre field of mammoth clover which was just beginning to bloom: "Do you mean to tell me that there are enough bumble bees in the whole county to get around to every one of the fifty or sixty little blossoms (which go to make up one big blossom) in this ten-acre field and thus start a clover seed to growing in each one, and do all this business before the blossoms begin to die? Not much!"

"It does look a little unreasonable," said I, "but I notice a few stalks just over there that for some reason are late and have not yet begun to bloom. Suppose you cover a hundred of these blossoms with some kind of a screen that will keep out not only the bumble bees, but all other insects, and then in the fall count the heads and seeds, after examining them very carefully, and see how much seed you will get, and then compare these with the same number of heads to which the insects have had free access."

"Oh," said he, "I am not going to that bother; it is too nonsensical."

"So it seems; but this is just what Darwin did when preparing to write his book on "Cross and Self-Fertilization of Plants." He covered one hundred heads of red clover with netting, counted the seeds, and then counted the seeds of a hundred heads right along side of them to which the insects had access. He found in these uncovered heads 2,720 clover seeds; in those covered with netting he found—not one. You will see a full account of it in the book mentioned, page 361.

"This simple experiment has been repeated by Professor Cook, of the Agricultural Department at Washington, and with the same results. You will find his report in Bulletin No. 26, Division of Entomology, page 87. Professor Beal, after investigating the subject quite thoroughly, came to the same conclusion, which you will find in full in his book entitled "Grasses of North America," pages 325–328. The New Zealand and Australian farmers tried to grow clover seed without bumble bees, they not being native of that country, and failed. In 1884 they shipped over a lot of bumble bees from England, and now, according to Thompson, "Insect Life," Vol. IV, page 157, they have increased so rapidly that the natives fear they will become a pest. So you see, my friend, that those who have gone to the trouble to sift the matter to the bottom are dead against you.

"But let us look into this matter for ourselves. Let us lie down a bit and watch what is going on about us. Notice first what great numbers of bumble bees come sailing in from every direction. See how busy they are, and how little time it takes them. Look at that big one over there. She puts her nib into one floret, or little flower, and seems to say, 'That's good'—into the next, and draws it out instantly. evidently some one has been there before and the honey is gone.   Thus she keeps on from morning to night, stopping only to visit her nest with a load.   And then see what honey bees are about us."

"Nonsense," said Job.   "Honey bees don't work on red clover."

"Keep still, will you, for two minutes and use your eyes.   There is one with three bands around her, evidently an Italian.   There's another.   There's hundreds of them in sight if you just look for them, all busy as only bees can be.   You will notice there are few, or none, of the little black bees here.   They don't seem to be able to reach down to the pollen."

"Well," said Job, "if that don't beat creation.   I never saw bees work on red clover before.   Did you bring them with you from town?"

"We don't often find honey bees," I replied, "on the first crop of common red, because the white and alsike clovers are plenty about the time it blooms, and the bees get the honey easier and quicker from these than from the deeper blossoms. You would not see them here to-day if it were not that the other clovers are drying up for want of rain.   You will find them on the red clover in the pastures where the cattle have kept it back from bloom- ing at the usual time.   But what else do you see?"

"Nothing but butterflies."

"Are they not poking their nibs down into these florets, and may they not help? But let us dissect a floret and see what we find.   Deep down in the tube we find the male and female parts of the flower. There is sex in all flowers.   The pollen, or male element, must either fall on the female parts, called ovules, or be placed on them.   In corn the fine dust of the tas- sels falls on the silk.   If you cut the tas- sel off a hill of corn standing by itself, you will have no ear.   If the tassels were be- low and the silk above, there could be no corn,   That is the precise situation, as you may see for yourself with the help of this small microscope, in all these florets. The male and female organs lie together, but the stamens, or the male organs, a half-dozen or more of them in each little floret, are shorter than the pistil, or the female, and the pollen, or fertilizing dust, from these would naturally fall down and away from the pistil were it not that the bees or butterflies poke their nibs in past them to the honey that lies below and carry the dust to the next flower."

"If all this be so," said Job, "why don't the first crop of red clover produce seed?"

"For the very good reason that the bees do not work on it. The nest of bumble bees does not carry a stock of workers through the winter as does the common hive bee. The queens alone survive. They start out in the spring, build their nests, lay eggs, and proceed to rear their young. For this reason there are comparatively few of them seen in the fields when the first crop of red clover is coming into bloom and ready to set seeds. The honey

bees have plenty to do on the white clover and alsike, and later, on the linden and
bass wood, hence they do not bother with
red clover except at times when no other
flowers are available.

"The first crop of red clover, however,
does produce some seed.   Where red clover and timothy are grown together and
the timothy cut for seed, there will generally be found more or less clover seed
with it, and this comes from the first crop.
The reason, therefore, that the first crop
of red clover does not produce seed, is because the insects do not fertilize it.   In
point of fact, if you will examine a crop
of mammoth clover carefully, you will see
that the earliest heads of it are comparatively barren of seed.   This is one of the
reasons which lead farmers to pasture off
mammoth clover up to the 10th or 15th of
June.   Even then I never expect a full
crop of clover seed of any kind if the season is such as to favor a continuous growth
of white clover through the season. There
are not usually, it is quite true, sufficient

bumble bees to do the business, and we must depend on the help of the Italian honey bees if we expect a full crop of seed."

"Suppose, then, I were to pasture off the red clover until the middle of June. Would I get seed from the first crop?"

"Certainly, if other conditions were right."

"Since we are on this seed business, how am I to know whether a crop of clover seed is worth cutting?"

"By examining it, of course. If you have a full stand and an average of twenty grains to the head, it is generally safe to figure on a crop of about two bushels, if it can all be saved. If it averages thirty grains per head, I would feel safe in counting on a crop of three bushels. I would rather pasture than cut a crop of less than two bushels."

"When would you cut this crop?'

"When it is ripe; when the heads are all turned a dark brown."

"What is the best machine to use?"

"An old-fashioned self-raker. These are becoming scarce now, and where one cannot be had readily, I would use an ordinary binder, removing the binding apparatus and putting on a flax attachment, which would cost about $5.00. Others remove the binding apparatus, leaving the deck board and dropper, and bolting on the latter a three-inch board of the same thickness, extending eighteen inches to the rear. Then bolt a piece of iron half an inch wide, a quarter of an inch thick, and eighteen inches long, on the rear end of this dropper and at right angles to it, bending in a semi-circle upward to the driver's seat and to the end of which they attach a small rope or cord, bringing it up through a small pulley fastened on the top of the machine and above the elevating rollers, and extending to a treadle on the footboard in front of the driver's seat. Wood pieces are put in in lieu of the iron parts that have been removed with the binding apparatus. In this way the clover can be cut and dumped in such gavels as

seems best.   Where the stand is thin, it
can be cut with the ordinary mower and
raked in small windrows, taking care to
rake it only when slightly damp, especially after it has had two or three days of
hot sun.   Of late the inventive genius of
the American has supplied us at small cost
with the buncher which can be attached
to the mowing machine."

"What about threshing it?"

"The old rule is to let it lie two or three
weeks until there comes at least one good
rain.   I doubt the wisdom of the rule.
When clover had to be flailed off with a
birch limb, as it did when I was a boy,
and hulled with an old-fashioned threshing machine with the cylinder boxed, that
was the proper way.   With a modern clover huller it is quite different.   If the
mammoth, for example, is allowed to lie
long, it is liable to be injured by hail, or
if wet weather comes about the last of
August or the first of September, while it
lies in the gavels, the under seed may
sprout.   The weather in the season or

mammoth is hot and dry, and I would thresh it as soon as it becomes dry and brittle. A rain or two will not hurt it in the least, but rather help.

"It is more difficult to handle a second crop of the common red. When it is ready for cutting the days are getting cool and short. I would cut as soon as the heads were all brown and would thresh it in a couple of weeks, if possible. Clover cannot be hulled when it is at all damp, and hence in the latter part of the season six hours' work of the huller in a day is about all that we can expect.

"The most serious difficulty in growing clover seed is that of getting a huller when you want it. The threshermen are busy with grain and will not usually stop to hull clover seed. They, therefore, compel the clover grower to await their leisure, and it is often a question whether he will do this at a great loss or stack his seed clover, top it out with slough grass, and wait until zero weather in the winter before attempting to thresh. Often it is either this or

buy a huller himself, and where he is en-
gaged in growing clover seed largely, or
a few farmers in one neighborhood are
doing so, this is the proper thing to do.
In fact, it is often the only way of securing the seed after it has been grown."

I do not think Job Barshear believed
more than half that I told him that day,
so hard it is to change the fixed opinions
of farmers. I had the satisfaction of knowing, however, that the facts pointed out
are such as will be clearly before him all
summer long, and I feel confident that
when he has had time to see for himself
and turn the thing over in his mind for a
year or two, he will come to my opinion.
The facts, as I have stated them, are all
within reach of every farmer, and he can
demonstrate their correctness for himself
with very little trouble and no expense.

CHAPTER XI.

SATAN IN THE CLOVER FIELD.

IT IS written in a very old part of the good Book, that when the good people came together Satan came also among them, or words to that effect. When the clovers come into any country, county or state in great tracts of broad acres, when they grow freely on every part of every farm, then, not only one, but many satans, come in the form of various kinds of ravenous, and otherwise destructive insects, attacking the root, the stalk, the leaf, the seed, the flower; and not content with this, follow it into the barn and devour the dry hay.

More than eighty species of insects have already been noted, living to a greater or less extent on the clovers, and every year or two some new clover satan, or adversary, is discovered. The most of these, such as various kinds of grasshoppers, leaf hoppers, butterflies, etc., are not peculiar to the clovers, while others do but little damage and need not be mentioned here. In a contest with any of them, the farmer is to a great extent powerless on account of their wide distribution and in-credible capacity of increase in a very short period of time, and must rely, in his controversy with these satans, on improved methods of rotation, and on their natural enemies, the parasites, which by a wise and merciful dispensation of the Giver of all good, in due time, always hold them in check and prevent the total destruction of the crop. Nevertheless, it is very im-portant for the clover grower to under-stand the nature and habits of the most destructive and dangerous of them, and to know the little satans, or adversaries, when he sees them.

If you are walking through the clover pasture some Sabbath afternoon in the summer time and looking, perhaps, for four-leaved clovers, thinking about farm matters instead of more sacred themes, you may sometimes notice the leaves of the white clover folded together on the central axis. You stop and say to yourself: "It cannot be dry enough, or hot enough yet to wilt clover." You pick off a leaf, open it out, and if your eyes are very good, you may notice from one to twenty little orange-colored maggots busy at work. If so, you have come across, perhaps for the first time, the clover leaf midge. It may have been there every year, but you did not notice it before. Fortunately, it is not a bad pest, and seldom attacks the red clovers, and then only the lower leaves, on which it produces galls, doing on this very little damage. The grazing of cattle and its exposed situation on the leaf, rendering it liable to the ravages of birds and parasites peculiar to itself, all stand in the way of its increase to any dangerous extent.

You are making the first crop of red clover hay, and you notice that some of the stalks pull o..t and are pushed on by the mower. You get off and examine, and find the stalks pull up easily, as though something were the matter with the root, and you wonder what it is. You do not think much about it, however, and suppose these stalks died prematurely in some way. The second crop starts, but it does not look just right, and much of it stops growing about the time it ought to head out. You now begin to wonder what is the matter with the clover.

There is matter enough. One of the meanest of the clover satans has been at work in the field. Its name is the clover root borer. As a matter of curiosity merely, we might say to you that the wise men call it "Hylesinus Trifolii." You will like the name of clover root borer best because it exactly describes its work. That you may understand it better, I give you an illustration:

Last spring the bug (marked "d" in the illustration) after awakening from its winter sleep, found a stalk of yearling clover in your field. It wanted a home in which

to rear its young. It bored a hole in the crown of the root, ate out a very large cavity, and said with the Psalmist:

"This is my rest; here still I'll stay,
For I do like it well."

proceeded to lay a number of eggs, and died, having fulfilled its evil mission. In about a week the young satans hatched out, found plenty of good living handy in that clover crown, and as they grew, proceeded to bore down into the roots of the infested stalk (marked "a" in the illustration), and if you will look closely, you will find them about the end of the root by the fall of the year. You can scarcely see the little rascals in the root, and so I have given you at "b" a magnified illustration, while "c" shows the form in which they come through the winter ready to hatch out in the spring and begin on the crop you have sown this year. · They never do any harm to the young clover for the reason that it has not yet started when they begin their work in the spring.

What now is to be done? Nothing, that I know of, except to plow up that clover field and let the birds, the mice, the gophers, and the moles eat the grubs before they have time to hatch out the next spring. The only loss, therefore, from this pest is the seed crop and part of the fall pasture; loss enough, it is true, to the man who needs money, as most of us do. It is, however, a blessing in disguise sometimes, to compel a farmer to plow up his clover in the fall of the second year and harvest his crop of nitrogen, gathered from the atmosphere, before it is washed out of the soil by rains.

You may notice some day when you are in the clover field, certain leaves with a circular disc eaten out of them about the shape of the marks that a cow makes on a blue grass pasture when she has put her head through a barb wire fence from the adjoining field, or perhaps the lane, and shaved off everything clean as far as her tongue can reach. This is the work of another beetle that seems to be too lazy to move its body, and has a neck well hinged. I know of no common name for it. Scientists call it the "flavescent clover beetle." I wish they would choose a simpler name. You will hardly find it if you look for it, as it will drop off the leaf and hide if you make the slightest movement. It is, therefore, scarcely necessary to illustrate it, or even to describe it further. It is not likely to do much damage anyhow, and I tell you about it to set you to looking sharp when you happen to see these circular discs cut in the center or on the margin of the leaves of red clover

You may, perhaps, have noticed among the winter wheat, timothy, or the yarrow or thistles that grow in the pasture, a plant here and there which has broken down before producing seed. On examining it you will likely find it full of little grubs that are eating their way down, and thus causing the plant to dwindle and die. If the clover stood up as straight as the above mentioned plants, you would find the same insect at work here and there

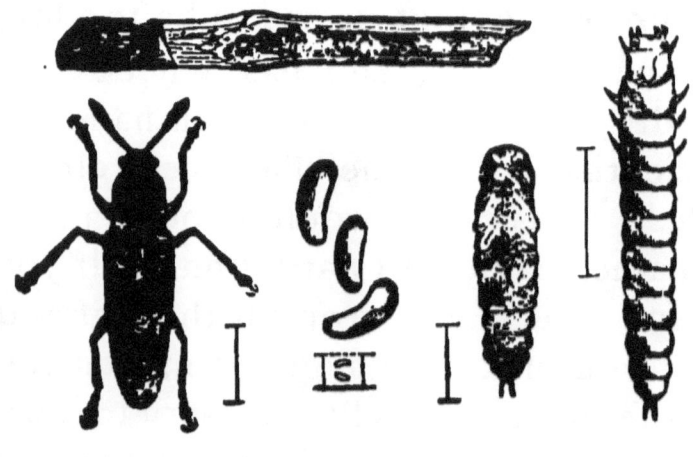

FIG. II.   THE CLOVER STEM BORER.

among the larger clovers. This is the work of the clover stem borer. It is, as above stated, not peculiar to clover, nor is it likely to become a very serious pest, and the less likely, because it has, like most other pests of this kind, a number of parasites which keep it in check.   However, to gratify your curiosity and set you seeing things, I give an illustration (see Fig. II) for which I am indebted to the Department of Agriculture.

The Germans, however, have given us a very destructive clover satan.   (Devil, I would say, if it were not that the preachers might think I was poaching on their preserves and using profane language, though I never could understand why it was profane to call Satan by his Anglo-Saxon name.)   This pest may give us very serious trouble before many years, although so far as I know it has not yet appeared west of Ohio nor at any great distance from streams, or large bodies of water.   Its first appearance on this continent was in Canada in 1853, in New York in 1881, at Buffalo in 1884, in northeastern Ohio along the lake shore in 1891, and more recently at Cincinnati.   Should it

reach the great clover fields of the West
in a few years, there will be a lot of very
sad and sorry farmers. Unlike other clover pests, it is active both in its worm, or
larval stage, and in its mature, or beetle
stage, and literally eats up in one or other
form, every part of the clover plant above
ground. The following illustration will
give the reader an idea of its capacity for

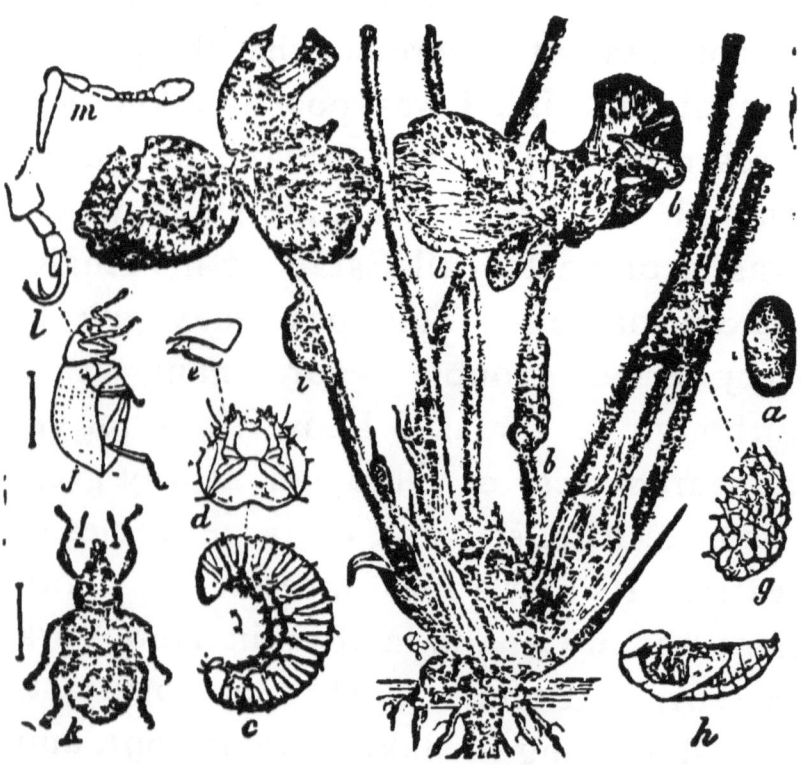

FIG. III. THE CLOVER LEAF BEETLE.

mischief, and he will not wonder after he studies it why we want the preachers' permission to call it a clover devil.

In the illustration, "a" represents an egg greatly enlarged; the various "b's" represent the different stages of growth while feeding on the leaf; "c" represents the young larva; "d" the head as viewed from beneath; "e" represents its jaws enlarged, both showing the capacity of the pest for mischief; "g" and "h" the pupa; "j" the side view of the beetle, and "k" a back view of the same slightly reduced from the natural size; and "l" and "m" the foot and antenna enlarged. For this illustration we are indebted to Dr. Riley.

The common name of this satan is "the clover leaf beetle." The scientists give it the jaw-breaking name of "Phytonomus punctatus," and when you meet in the reports of experiment stations with this jaw-breaker, you will understand that it means simply the clover leaf beetle. It begins its work early in the spring, commencing

on the young leaves of the clover about
as soon as they appear.   It is waiting for
them and hungry, but they are young yet
and the farmer does not notice its work
particularly until about May or June,
when he will see the larvæ eating the
leaves as represented in the illustration,
feeding sidewise on the edge of the leaf
on the underside.   Until he learns how to
observe them, he will not see the beetles
themselves--only their work.   They saw
him first and dropped to the ground and
hid, as if troubled with a guilty conscience.
After sundown they climb up the stalk,
and while the good man is asleep, dream-
ing, perhaps, of barns and sheds filled with
well cured clover, and a stack or two in
the field for which there was no room,
millions of jaws are busy at work cutting
down his clover and utterly destroying it
in advance, compelling him to take his
corn cutter and find winter forage for his
cattle in the corn field.

The mature beetles appear in July and

August, and proceed at once to eat up whatever clover the larvæ or worms have left.   They lay their eggs, and another crop of larvæ appear in September, change to pupæ in October, and emerge as beetles in November.   Some of these lay eggs from which larvæ hatch and hibernate while quite small in the old clover stems.   Others hibernate as beetles, lay their eggs the following spring.   The female lays from two to three hundred eggs in the stem of the clover, which it usually punctures for that purpose.   The larvæ, or worms, are constitutionally hungry, and consume every part of the plant above the surface of the earth.

It will be seen at once that the farmer has very slight chance of success in entering into a contest with this sort of pest. Spraying with Paris green would no doubt kill them, as it would other pests; but who would go to work to spray a clover field? The best thing to be done is to keep your eyes open, and when the field is found to be infested in May, plow it up and put it in corn.　In one sense there is a loss in this, but it is a loss that would have to be endured anyhow, and it is better to have a good crop of corn, than disappointed hopes in the way of a clover crop.

The most common of all the pests, however, that have yet appeared in the Western states, is the clover seed midge, quite common, indeed, in recent clover years, as far west as northern Iowa, but of which nothing has been heard lately.　It will no doubt, however, appear in increasing numbers as soon as the practice of growing clover seed has become quite general for two or three years in succession. That our readers may recognize it when it does come, we give three figures illustrating the insect.　Figure IV is a large back view of the male with scales stripped off in order to show the structure more clearly; and Figure V the female, while Figure VI represents the maggot, or larva enlarged, and seen from the underside of the leaf.　The

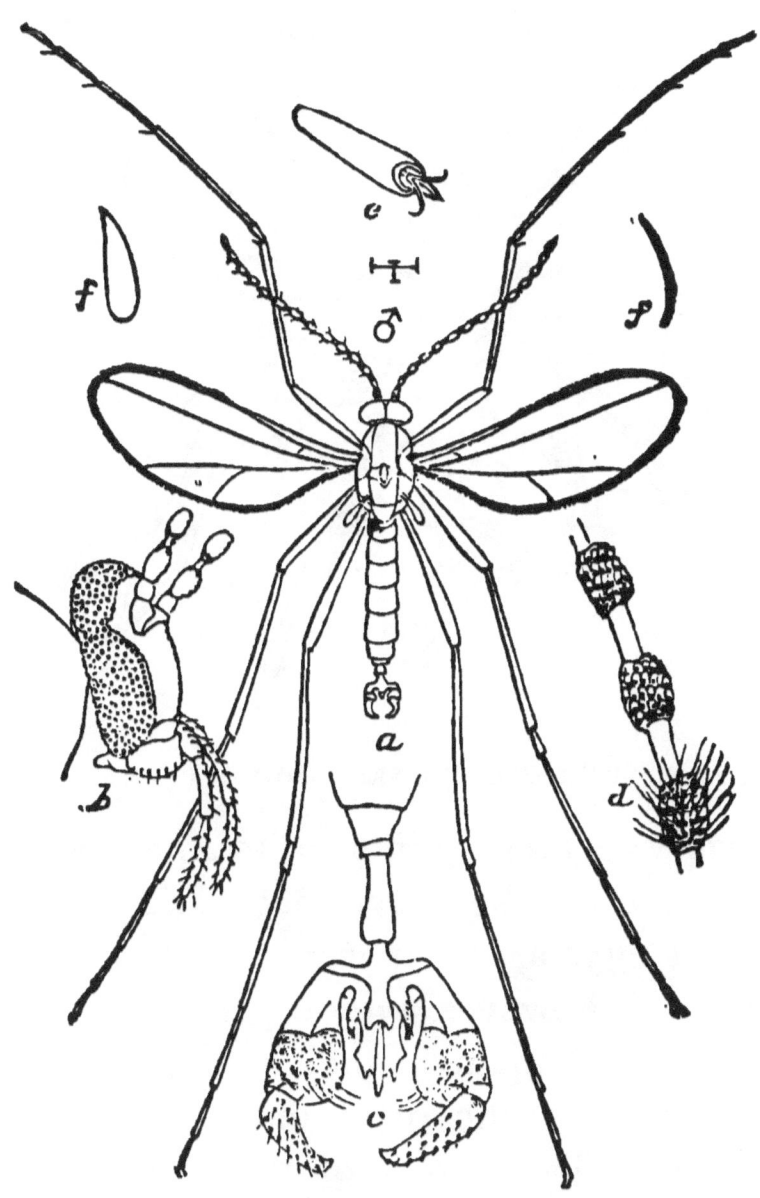

FIG. IV. THE CLOVER SEED MIDGE (MALE).

main difference between this pest and the clover leaf midge, first mentioned, is that

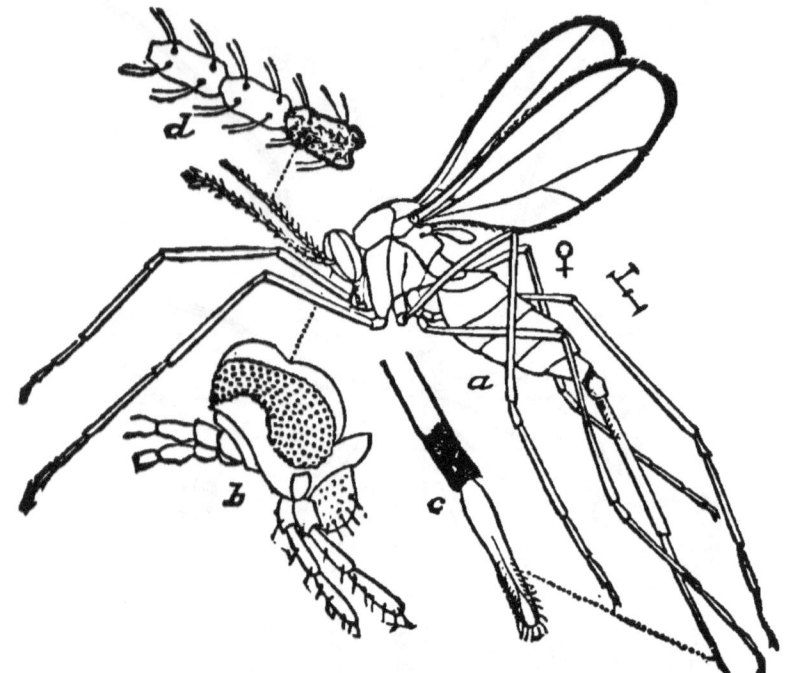

FIG. V. THE CLOVER SEED MIDGE (FEMALE).

it has two more joints in its antennæ, or feelers, than the clover leaf midge, and that its eggs are somewhat larger. You will need, however, a good pair of eyes to see either of them, as their average length is only about the one-hundredth part of an inch. The female of the clover seed midge appears about the time the heads of the clover appear, and before the bloom, which stage of development occurs in central Iowa toward the latter part of May, and earlier or later south or north, according to latitude. In other words,

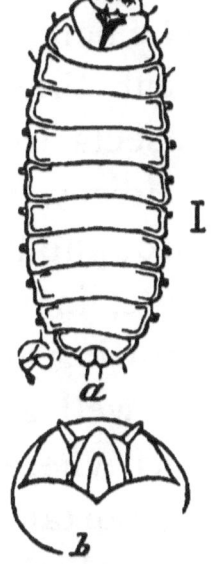

the egg is deposited before the bloom appears, but after the head is formed. By the time the eggs are hatched into worms, the mouth of the floret is open, and the maggots work their way through the mouth down to the seed, feeding on it while it is yet in the dough state, after the manner of the wheat midge so common forty years ago.

FIG. VI
THE LARVA. By the time the clover is fit to cut, these maggots wriggle out of the heads that have been accidentally fertilized by the bumblebees, pass into the ground, and the mature insects again appear about the time the second crop of clover is ready for their mischief. It is this last crop that does the damage, making, where they are at all numerous, a seed

crop on the common red clover unprofit-
able, if not, in fact, impossible.

How to deal with this pest is a problem.
It could be held in check readily enough
if the corn, and the inclination of the farmer, and of the farmers all over the neighborhood, would lead them to cut their
first crop very early before the insects are
ready to leave the head. This, however,
under conditions prevailing throughout
the entire country is impracticable, inasmuch as it would require the mowing at
this early date, of pastures as well as
meadows. However, in sections where
clover seed growing is not an important
feature of agriculture, comparatively little
damage is done. By the time the pest
has become general and entirely destructive of the seed crop, parasites appear in
great numbers. One of these belongs to
the same family as the joint worm fly, un-
dergoes its transformation within the seed,
gnaws a hole through it large enough to
let it out shortly after the maggots have
left the seed to go into the ground. An-

other parasite stays with the midge, goes into the ground with it, and emerges when full grown from the cocoon, which contains a dead midge.

In sections where clover seed is an important crop, the thing to do is to drop out the common red and use the mammoth. This variety, as the reader already knows, is from two to three weeks later than the common red, hence its heads have not appeared when the midge fly is getting in its work, and the seed is all formed and ready to cut before the second crop of flies are ready to begin operations.

I wish to caution the reader against buying clover seed containing the midge. Miss Eleanor Omerod, of St. Albans, England, one of the highest authorities on entomology, or "bugology," states that the midge has been found in American seed exported to England; and Professor Beal, in his work on grasses, page 391, says that the larvæ (of the full brood, of course) have been found on seed in the market, and he thus explains the rapid distribution of this pest. Seedsmen will require to be particularly watchful in case the midge becomes common again, as it no doubt will, and thus protect farmers against its ravages. The farmer who grows seed and sells to his neighbor, will do well to provide himself with a magnifying glass sufficiently large to detect any kind of impurity; and whether he buys his seed, or grows it, it will be well before sowing, to steep it in water at a temperature of 120 degrees, and afterward at a temperature of 135 degrees, thus applying what is known as the Jenson process so effective in destroying smut on oats.

The reader will pardon me if I call his attention to another clover satan well known in the East, and which, some years ago, became common as far west as the state of Iowa, called by the scientists "Grapholipha interstinctana," but which will be better understood if I call it by the common name of the clover seed caterpillar. That the reader may recognize it on sight, I give an illustration for which I am indebted to the Iowa Agricultural Experiment Station at Ames.

It is a moth (letter "d" of the illustration) which appears about the last of May, and in the short space of a month goes

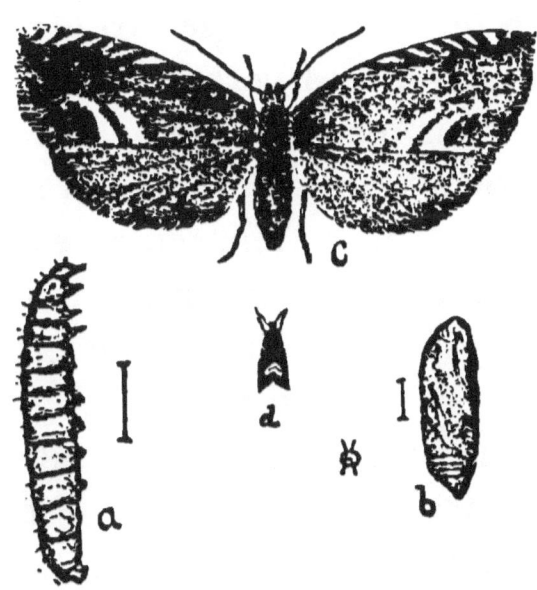

FIG. VII.

THE CLOVER SEED CATERPILLAR.

through its larval growth, "a," and begins to spin a cocoon. In order that our readers may more readily distinguish this pest, they will notice at "c" the moth greatly magnified. The damage done by this insect, however, is purely to the seed crop. It does not bother the seed, but it eats into the florets, or small flowers, of which t : head is composed, and later into the seed vessels of the floret, causing the florets to dry up and the seeds to shell prematurely from their receptacles. There seems to be at least three broods in the latitude of Iowa, and perhaps four.

This insect will do no great harm to the clover grower who is not counting on a seed crop. The remedies for the clover seed grower consist in, first, a rotation of crops, plowing under the clover every second year—a good thing, by the way, on general principles, caterpillar or no caterpillar; second, close fall pasturage so as to leave the field free from vegetation in the fall, and avoiding putting manure on clover fields which he does not intend to plow under the next spring; third, early cutting. This pest, like most others, has numerous parasites which in due time reduce it to such numbers as render it comparatively harmless.

One of the most annoying adversaries of the farmer and clover plant is the clover hay worm, which eats up the hay in the barn or stack after the farmer has bestowed all his labor and care upon it. The

following illustration, for which we are indebted to Professor Cook, will enable the

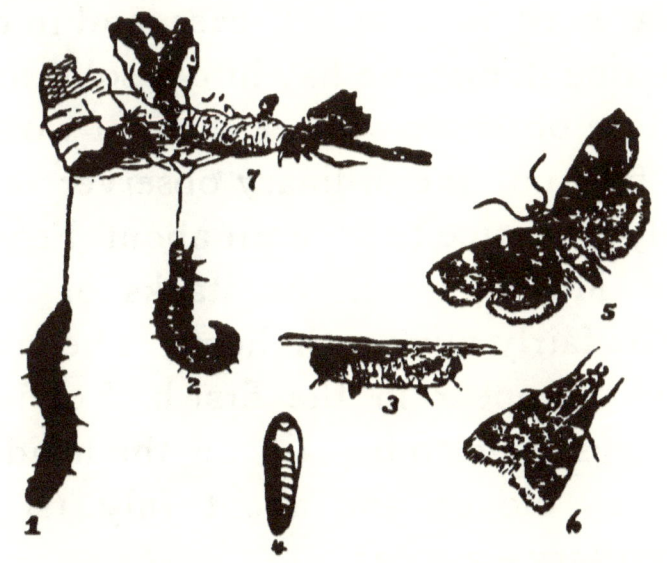

FIG. VIII.   THE CLOVER HAY WORM.

reader to identify it, although after it has
once established itself on his farm he will
not have much need of the illustration.

In this, Figures 1 and 2 represent the
larvæ suspended by threads of their own
spinning; Figure 3 the cocoon, which may
be found by thousands around the barn
in which the clover hay worm has been
doing its work; 4 the chrysalis; 5 represents the moth with outspread wings; 6 the
moth at rest; and Figure 7 the larva con-

cealed in a case of silk which it has spun. The eggs are laid on the clover. The larvæ work in a silken case, and in constructing it, mat the hay into a solid mass. A close observer will see them at work in the fall, but the ordinary observer is not likely to notice them until about February or March, when the stacks or barns will be fairly alive with them. The moths begin to appear in the first half of June; the eggs seem to be laid on the heads of growing clover, and about July 1st the young larvæ appear.

I have had a good deal of correspondence for several years with isolated farmers whose buildings are infested with this pest. Some of them write me that moisture is quite essential to the development of the worm, and hence only the lower two feet of the stack or mow are greatly damaged. Some claim that by making a stack bottom of timber, logs or rails, and raising the stack about two feet above the ground, they suffer little damage; while others claim that even when

the hay is put into a mow entirely free
from moisture, the worm does its work
with about the same facility. Inasmuch
as the insect appears to stay closely by
buildings that are once infested, the only
remedy of which I know is to burn all
stack bottoms before the moths appear,
and to haul all affected hay out of the
barn and burn it as early in the spring as
possible before the insects have left the
hay to spin their cocoons. Some farmers
have taken the precaution, and with good
results, of sprinkling the lower two or
three feet of their hay when first put in
the mow with lime.

I have been frequently asked whether
the moths will injure the cattle that feed
on this worm infested hay. Inasmuch as
a sensible cow will not take very kindly
to hay bound together with the silken
bands of these cocoons, I do not think
there is much danger.

I have dwelt at length on these various
insect pests, because with the increase in
clover growing, which is surely coming,

some or all of these insects will in time
appear; and while the farmer cannot do
much in the way of destroying them, he
can, by a careful study of their nature and
habits, and by putting his knowledge into
practice, avoid much serious loss.   The
main dependence, however, is in their natural enemies, the parasites peculiar to
each, which after all is the main protec-
tion the farmer has against any sort of insect pests, and in a judicious rotation of
crops which will enable him to make the
best use possible of infested fields.

CHAPTER XII.

THE CLOVERS IN THE PERMANENT PASTURE.

IT REQUIRES about two acres of the ordinary permanent pastures, even in the best portions of the United States, to keep well a steer weighing a thousand pounds, seven months in the year, or from May 1st to December 1st. In very many sections three acres are required, while three acres of good wild prairie grass will keep a steer of the same weight five months in an equally thrifty condition. It may surprise our readers to know that in Great Britain and Ireland, on their best lands, naturally no better than the prairie lands of the United States, one statute, or American acre, will keep a steer of the same weight ten or eleven months in the year. It is quite true that the British farmer is not subject to the severe drouths that sometimes prevail in the United States, that the climate is more equable, the rainfall, while no greater, is more equally distributed, and that there is no danger of grasses being killed by hard freezing; but on the other hand the clovers, with the exception of white and alsike, do indifferently well with him, and blue grass is of comparatively little value; in fact, neither Great Britain nor Ireland are blue grass countries. The question arises, how may our permanent pastures be so improved that they may approximate in yield and quality to the permanent pastures of the Old World?

I fully believe that the capacity of our permanent pastures may be increased fifty per cent., if not in fact doubled, and that with very slight expense beyond the application of brains. However, before any improvement is likely to be made, the farmer must first understand that grasses, with the exception of the clovers, do not enrich land. It is true that land becomes enriched while in pasture, first, by the gradual accumulation of humus or vegetable mold in the soil, thus modifying its texture and enabling it the better to withstand drouth when put in corn or the cereals; and second, by the gradual but slow accumulation of available potash and phosphoric acid in the soil, partly the result of disintegration, and partly by the action of the grass roots, which, as heretofore explained, secrete an acid in which these elements become soluble in pure water.

Apart from these two sources of fertility, pastures composed of the true grasses add nothing to the fertility of the soil. It is the experience of farmers in the Eastern states that when live stock are sold from the permanent pasture and no manure returned, these pastures gradually fail, the grasses becoming thinner and coarser, and weeds taking their place, then thorns and brush, and finally, in the course of time, the pasture becomes a forest. If the true grasses added to the fertility of the soil, this could not occur. Hence the farmer must get into his head a clear conception of an ideal permanent pasture. It is not a pasture that grows luxuriantly in May and June, suspends growth until after the fall rains, and then resumes it until freezing weather. This describes the majority of permanent pastures in the United States, and it is little wonder that requires from two to three acres of them to sustain a thousand pounds of live stock seven months.

The ideal pasture is made up of the greatest possible variety of grasses, true and artificial. By artificial grasses we mean the clovers. These grasses should have, to as great an extent as possible, different periods of blooming, so that from the middle of April until the ground freezes up, there should be a constant succession of young shoots, and from early in May until October, of bloom. In short, the permanent pasture should have more grasses than can find room to spread themselves, or make their greatest efforts at any one period of the year. It is impossible, under American conditions, to provide a pasture of this kind without making the largest possible use of the clovers, and the failure to maintain these clovers in the permanent pasture is the real reason why, as a rule, it has such comparatively little productive capacity.

I am met at once with the argument that blue grass will strangle the larger clovers and take complete possession of the ground. That is true. Blue grass is essentially a monopolist, but like all other monopolists, it, in the end, defeats its own selfish purposes, and hence must be controlled for its own good, as well as for the good of the public. The welfare of the blue grass in the pasture requires that about once every two or three years it be thoroughly ripped up with a disk, or better, with a disk drill, and timothy and the larger clovers be resown. It is of no use to sow them on the surface and allow them to take their chances. As I have said before, the clovers must be covered, and a thorough disking, followed by harrowing, or drilling in with a disk, is essential to success. Wherever I have known this method to be tried it has added from fifty to one hundred per cent. to the productive capacity of the pasture, and there is no reason why the method should not be adopted on every farm where the object in maintaining a permanent pasture is to secure the largest amount of forage per acre. I have not adopted this method on my own pastures for the reason that it would interfere with the gathering of the crop of blue grass seed, which is one of my annual crops. Nevertheless, in wet years and on portions subject to overflow or wash from higher lands, the clover and timothy put in their appearance, even on a blue grass sod of fourteen years' standing.

Where this course has been followed, we begin to approximate the ideal permanent pasture, in which orchard grass begins to make growth early in April, according to the season, blue grass following a few days later and heading out in the latitude of central Iowa from the 27th of April to the 10th of May, followed in a few days by the heads of the orchard grass, then by the bloom of the white clover, followed during the latter end of May by the red, and this again in about two or three weeks by the mammoth, at which time the blue grass is ripening its seed and suspending growth, in ordinary years, until the fall rains come. During this period of suspended growth the clovers are in the fullness of their bloom, followed by a rank growth of orchard grass in August, and by the time the clovers have ripened their seed the blue grass is beginning its fall work, which it continues without interruption until the ground freezes. Hence, we have a continuance through every day of the summer, whether wet or dry, hot or cold, of fresh herbage and bloom. Clovers thus maintained in the permanent pasture, in spite of the blue grass, fill the sod with nitrogen and make it possible for the blue grass itself to attain to a far greater luxuriance than when it is allowed to occupy the soil to the exclusion of everything else but white clover. More than that, the clovers balance the ration of the stock grazing on the pasture, adding to it abundantly the flesh-forming elements, thus not only largely increasing the yield, but very greatly improving its quality as far, at least, as young and growing stock is concerned.

To my mind, one of the greatest defects in our modern system of agriculture is this failure to secure an ideal permanent pasture by the free use of the larger clovers. While blue grass is a valuable servant, it is no safer to allow it to have its own way, than it is the valuable horse, or the promising son or daughter. No man is master of the science of clover growing until he has learned to make use of the larger clovers to the largest possible extent in his permanent pasture.

I can well imagine the thoughtful readers whose prairie land has not as yet been all broken out, or who may have corners of fields, or broken portions of his farm that are as yet untouched by the plow and covered with native grasses, asking the question: If the larger clovers can be reseeded in as tough and unyielding a sod as blue grass, why not sown on prairie? And the question at once arises, Why not? I have been greatly interested for some years past in watching the gradual extension of red clover on both sides of a road winding through a piece of wild prairie. It began with a lone stalk here and there some years ago, and has now extended until for two or three rods on either side, the prairie has every appearance of a rich clover field. The first seed was evidently dropped by passing teams. The sod had been broken by farmers turning out with their wagons in muddy times, or by cattle driven along the roadside. The seeds had been dropped from wagons loaded with hay, or in some other way, and wherever the sod was broken and the seed planted the clovers grew. Why not, then, break the sod in the way above suggested, and at the same time sow the clover? While

I have never tried it, I believe it is entirely practicable for any farmer having wild
prairie, in sections where clover growing is a
success, and in normal years, to seed down
unbroken prairie with common red or
mammoth clover, and in the course of two
or three years transform it into an old
clover sod which, when turned under, will
yield a bumper crop of corn the first year.
I do not say that this will succeed in sections of the country where clover growing
is an experiment, but I do maintain that
in clover sections in ordinary years clover
will be as willing to grow where it is sown
purposely and under the same conditions
as it.is where it is sown by accident. Of
course we shall be met with the old, old
story that the wild nature must be taken
out of the land by breaking it up in the
orthodox way and growing a number of
crops of grain. This idea is firmly fixed
in the minds of a good many farmers and
it is useless to argue with them or show
them that it is a hoary myth with no foundation in fact, whatever. I simply ask them

to open their eyes and see what is going on about them. There is no more wildness in prairie land along the roadside than there is far afield. Clover grows whenever it has an opportunity; that is, when the sod is broken in any way and the seed planted along the roadside. Why will it not grow all over the prairie under the same conditions? Is it not easier to use a disk drill that will rip up the soil and plant the seed at the same time, or a sharp disk, well weighted, and followed with the seed, 'and harrowed, than to pay some man for the expense of breaking and stirring, and be out the use of the field for a year? Why not use the help that comes to you through the clover plant and take the easy way and proffered help of nature in transforming the wild prairie into a cultivated field, with all its stored fertility intact and supplemented by the fertility which clover brings? I have seeded wild prairie to clover by simply hauling over it second crop clover in which there was too little seed to pay for threshing, and

allowing the cattle to eat what they wanted and the wind to blow the rest where it
would, and without disking or drilling.
Why not take a hint from nature's method
and save time and labor in transforming a
wild prairie into a permanent pasture by
the use of clover?

CHAPTER XIII.

THREE CLOVER HARVESTS IN ONE.

I HAD a very pleasant call the other day from young Job Barshear. After saying that he guessed that the bumblebees and Italians had evidently got in their best work on his trial field of mammoth clover, he said:

"That dream did father more good than all your writing, and he allowed me to sow ten acres just to see whether clover is all that it is cracked up to be; but he still sticks to it that there are not enough bumblebees and Italians in the whole county to fertilize the bloom in that one field. It's done, though. Something has done it, as the heads are all full and I am going to have a fine crop of clover seed. Now, what I want to know is, whether I can get a crop like it on this same field next year, and if not, what am I to do with it this fall or next spring?"

I like the looks of young Job. He seems to me to be a very fair type of thousands of farm boys who are tired of this everlasting grind of growing corn, oats, wheat, flax, corn, wheat, oats, flax, year after year without change from a grain to a grass crop; tired of hard work with little profit, and who would like to break away from the old methods, to get out of the ruts if their parents would only let them, or give them a little encouragement. These boys are not satisfied with the county paper, the singing-school and the lyceum, but really want to read, think and·act for themselves, or else get off the farm.

I know just how they feel, for I have been in their shoes. I would like to hold these boys on the farm, and yet I know that the best of them will not stay there until they have something to think about that promises them a dollar somewhere, to be made by thinking as well as working; and so I said:

"You had better harvest your three crops."

"Three crops!" said young Job.

"Yes, three crops—a crop of seed, a crop of humus, and a crop of nitrogen or fertility."

"I am going to harvest the seed crop, sure," he replied; "but I don't even guess what you mean by harvesting a crop of humus and a crop of nitrogen. You are joking, are you not?"

"Not in the least, but in dead, sober, serious earnest, as I am always when I talk to you boys. Let me explain. The trouble with your father's land was not that it was literally worn out, but that it was exhausted to a point that continuous grain crops did not pay. The good Lord always seems to me to have a special care of farmers, because they live closer to nature than do other people, nature being one of the books through the study of which He reveals Himself to man; and He does not allow even the worst soil robbers to rob the soil of all its fertility. He keeps

the most of it locked up as your mother
did the pies and cakes when you were a
little boy, telling you "they were laid over
for meddlers"—at least that is what my
mother used to say—and gives out the
potash and phosphoric acid, which makes
up the ash and are used in constructing
the frame work of the plant, slowly and
carefully. And when the lands become so
far worn out that it does not pay to raise
grain on them, he allows the farmer to
wrestle with the store bills and the mortgage until he gets to thinking right hard,
and is ready to learn, as you and your
father seem to be just now. By your
continuous raising of corn, oats, wheat,
flax, and then back to corn, or some similar rotation, you have wasted, worn out,
and used up the humus, or vegetable mold,
or that which makes a new soil look dark.
You may have often heard your father say
that the soil of the farm is a good deal
lighter in color than it was when first broken up from the prairie; that it washes
more, and does not stand either flood or

drouth as it used to. Next, you have used up the nitrogen, that element in the soil which feeds the plant with that sort of material that makes cattle grow in muscle, or flesh and blood. This element of plant food is soluble in the form in which the plant takes it up, and hence is easily washed away. This element of fertility is the commonest thing in all the world. We are living at the bottom of a sea of air supposed to be about forty miles deep, of which four-fifths is nitrogen; yet if you want to buy it in the shape of commercial fertilizers, it would cost you 15 cents per pound on the market."

"The great value of clover is, and in this all clovers are alike, that it is one of the few crops that can draw on this nitrogen of the air for the muscle-making sort of plant food. In this it is like peas and beans of all varieties, and a few other cultivated plants, which, however, it does not pay the general run of farmers to grow. I'll not tell you just now how it is that the clovers make use of this "free nitrogen," as the scientists call it. The fact that they do it is enough, coupled with the other fact that none of the true grasses, such as blue grass, timothy, or corn (which, as I have told you, is only a giant grass,) can. When the clover roots are turned under and decay, the plant gets the first feed out of them, the richness, so to speak, and the rest are slowly turned into vegetable mold or humus. Thus every clover plant when it reaches maturity is capable of furnishing three crops—a crop of seed, or, if of the medium variety, both hay and seed, a crop of nitrogen, and a crop of humus."

"You will save your clover seed crop first, of course. You will not have a great deal of aftermath, but you will have some. I don't count that as a crop. Pasture it off as close as you like if you need it; if not, no matter. Late this fall, or as late as you can safely undertake it, plow that field, and thus get ready to harvest the other two crops."

"Why not let it stand another year?" asked young Job.

"Because you are not likely to have a full stand next year. Mammoth clover is a biennial and dies at the end of the second year from planting. Only the hard seeds that failed to soak up enough water to justify them in starting to grow the first year will produce seed next. They are a year behind time. The rest will die, just as you and I will die when our time comes, and if your father and the neighbors tell you that they winter kill, do not believe them. They mean well but they are mistaken. In short, I would advise you not to pay any attention to what any man tells you about clover unless you know that he has succeeded in growing clover himself. The nitrogen which these dead plants and roots contain will, in the course of the next year, be washed down into the subsoil, or be leached out by heavy rains unless you harvest it, and like any other crop, it must be harvested when it is ready—not before nor after.

"When you cut your mammoth clover,

take as little of the stalk with it as you
can so as to secure the heads. It will save
you time and expense in threshing, and
the best place for the haulm is on the land.
I would spread the threshed haulm over
the thinner spots before plowing, and thus
increase the crop of humus. Next spring
when you go on this field with the disk to
prepare it for corn, you will find the soil
full of clover roots, which, together with
the haulm, will in their decay be converted into humus, or vegetable mold. This
is a crop which you cannot sell. It is not,
therefore, a cash crop. It has none the
less real value on that account. While
the roots are decaying they will keep
your soil from baking after heavy rains,
and in this way do much to conserve the
moisture; for it is the baked soil that dries
out rapidly in times of drouth. As these
roots decay they will fill it with manure,
scattered evenly as no mortal hand can do
it, and you will find that the soil will for
this reason stand more wet weather as well
as dry. By saving this crop as I have di-

rected, you will add humus enough to last it four years, and will even after that have more humus in the soil than there was when you first began sowing clover seed. For evidence of this see Farmers' Bulletin No. 78, Department of Agriculture. The experiments therein reported show conclusively that if a farmer will grow a crop of clover once in four years and harvest his crop of humus therefrom as above directed, his land will increase in the supply of this essential element from year to year, and in time will be restored to more than its virgin fertility.

"The third crop I wish you to harvest is the nitrogen. You can not see it, it is true, and it may seem to you like a dream crop. Neither can you see such a real thing as the air, or your mother's love, but you can see the effects of these and a dozen other invisible, intangible, but none the less real things that are a part of our daily life. This nitrogen which the plant uses in building up those elements that go to form flesh, hair and blood when fed to live stock, is partly in the roots and partly in the soil in which the clovers grew, or in rootlets, perhaps, so small that we cannot collect and weigh them; and the way to harvest this invisible, intangible substance is to prepare a first-class seed bed for the coming crop and let the roots of that crop gather up the fertility, whether in the decaying clover roots, or in the soil. Ever since men began to put brains into their farming, they have noticed this remarkable addition to the fertility of the soil that comes in the wake of a crop of clover, beans, peas, or any other of the legumes, which, by means of the little tubercles on the roots, take hold of the nitrogen of the atmosphere and place it, by their decay, where it can be used by other crops which are dependent wholly on the soil for their supply of flesh-formers.

"With a good season next year, you will have twenty-five bushels more corn per acre on this field than on similar land not clovered. If the season be poor, you may not have more than fifteen extra bushels, but in the two years you may reasonably count on forty bushels additional."

"Would you, then, advise me to take two crops of corn in succession?"

"Yes; if you did not sow a new field to clover last spring. If you did, then I would not, but would go on as fast as possible and get around your father's farm once with clover. When your land gets so rich that the oats will lie down in an average year, I would lengthen out the rotation by taking two crops of corn."

"I see. Now tell me why father and the rest of the grain raisers did not catch on to this long ago?"

"It is very easy to tell you that. Your father and the exclusive grain raisers came to a new country with little money and lots of faith in the richness of the soil. They had their lands to pay for, houses and stables to build, tools to buy, their families to keep, taxes to pay, and they had to make the most of it out of the land. They went to growing grain for sale, because it has the world for a market, and is a cash crop; and in this they did exactly right. They had, however, two wrong ideas. They thought that good prairie lands and the best class of timber lands would never wear out, and also that clover would not grow in a new country. They knew how to grow all kinds of grain, hence did not buy agricultural books nor read first-class agricultural papers. These were few and far between, and are too few now. When they got hold of an agricultural paper, so called, edited by a broken down lawyer, or some farmer who is running away from a mortgage and hiding under an editorial chair, or some business man who has no sympathy with farmers, they looked it over and said: "I know more about farming than that fellow does," and threw it aside; and in this again they were right. In ten or twelve years they exhausted largely the humus of the soil, and it began to bake and wash. It would stand neither wet weather nor dry. Hundreds of thousands of farmers were doing the same thing, and supplying from a virgin soil more grain than the world would take at paying prices, and the result was that with small crops and comparatively low prices, they began to fall behind. By this time, however, their habits had become fixed. They were in an intellectual rut and found it easier to jog along in that rut and lay the blame on the tariff, or the currency, or monopoly, than to take time to study and get at the real facts, and then make a heroic effort to get out of the rut and farm on right lines. It is in fellows like you who are young enough to learn and who are short on prejudices and long on energy and "get up," that the agriculture of the newer parts of the United States largely depends.

"If you will learn how to harvest these three crops this year, then take up the subject of crop rotations, and the place of clover in these, and, when you get on far enough to start in live stock and procure suitable buildings, take up the subject of clover in the ration, you will lay broad and deep the foundation of a happy and prosperous life as a farmer. If you do not read, study, and put correct theories in practice, but keep on as your fathers have done, growing grain, crop after crop, without a rotation having clover as a basis, or its starting and ending, you will have hard work and hard times right along, and finally become discouraged and miserable yourselves, blaming your misfortunes on others, and making yourselves a prey to political shysters of all parties who may want your votes to serve their own selfish purposes, aiming, in short, to make you stepping stones on which they may climb into the positions of power and influence. I don't say that clover is the only salvation, but I do say that it is one of the most efficient means by which the farmer can make himself a thoroughly self-respecting and influential member of any community where the soil is adapted to its growth, and that clover growing is closely connected with everything that is desirable in the life of an intelligent and prosperous farmer."

CHAPTER XIV.

CLOVERS IN THE ROTATION.

HOW to get out of a good thing all there is in it is one of the most important as well as difficult problems of life. If the men who have money, health, and reputation could only get all the good out of these that it is possible for them to obtain, this would be a very happy world, indeed, and we would all be much more unwilling even than we are now to exchange it for a better one.

To gather up and utilize to the best advantage all the fertility stored in the soil by a crop of clover in the two years of its growth, is one of the fine points of farming, and it can be done only by the adoption of a systematic rotation of crops, carefully mapped out according to the requirements of the location, climate, and markets of the farm. When once adopted it must be persistently followed if success is to be assured.

At the end of the second year's growth of clover, we have, in addition to the hay or seed crop, or both, a soil filled with a mass of roots about equal in weight to that of the hay crop, which, having fulfilled their mission, are ready to perish and bless succeeding crops by their death. It is important, therefore, that the clover crop should be immediately followed by a gross feeder, that is, a plant that draws largely from the soil—a crop that can take up the fertility as fast as it is transformed into available plant food by bacterial action, or in other words, by decay. Farmers do not always understand that vegetable matter, whether in the shape of clover or grass roots or farm yard manure, is not a plant food at all in that form, but merely the raw material out of which plant food is manufactured by bacteria.

There is no crop grown in the Eastern, Central, nor indeed in the Southern states,

so well adapted to this place in the rotation as corn. It is a gross feeder. It
makes its growth at a time when the rainfall and the temperature favor the greatest
activity among our friends—the bacteria
in the soil—that work for us, day and
night, all summer long, and without which
the most fertile land would become a desert. Hence, with clover to start with, the
first crop to follow should, on the majority of farms, be corn; and where the corn
crop is not used, its place should be taken
by potatoes. Corn is peculiarly adapted
for this purpose in the rotation, not only
because it is a gross feeder, but because
the time of planting permits either fall or
spring plowing; and if the former is practiced, gives ample time for the preparation of a seed bed and the killing of the
weeds by cultivation, by the use of the
disk or harrow from week to week, prior
to, and immediately following, the planting of the corn. It allows and requires
the continuous cultivation of the soil until
July 1st, and frequently later, and hence

affords the best opportunities for keeping it clear of weeds and hastening the process of decay, at the same time turning the products of decay into valuable grain and forage. On soils naturally good, that is, having in them the mineral elements necessary to plant growth, and in good condition at the beginning of the rotation, it will take two years to use up the fertility stored by a crop of clover. The first and second crops in the rotation, on lands naturally good, or that, if somewhat exhausted, by frequent croppings, have been brought up again to their natural standard of fertility, should be corn. On soils not up to the standard, it is advisable to take but one crop.

In sections adapted to the growth of winter wheat, a crop of that grain can be grown very cheaply by cutting the corn at the proper time, and immediately following with one of the disk drills which will sow and cover the wheat perfectly, even if by neglect the field has been allowed to become very weedy. This statement may be questioned by men who have had no experience; it will not be by those who have. The advantages of this method of growing winter wheat are: First, that it saves the expense of plowing and the preparation of the seed bed, the proper cultivation of the corn having prepared a very good seed bed in advance—a better one, in fact, than the farmer can give at that season of the year with any amount of other preparation on the land already in corn.

Second, this method immediately fills the soil with living roots which take up plant food about as rapidly as it is prepared by the action of the microbes in the soil at this season of the year, as the temperature falls rapidly after the 20th of September, microbic action always decreasing with the temperature.

Third, it reduces the cost of wheat-growing to the minimum, a very desirable thing when prices are low, as they are likely to to be in the average year. Timothy may be sown in the fall with the wheat, and clover the following February, on the surface, if the soil be full of moisture, or if it contains much clay. If there has been little precipitation in the winter, or if the soil be sandy or light loam, it is better to defer sowing the clover until the soil is in good condition in April, and then cover with a light harrow, even if the timothy seed has to be sown with it to repair the damage that harrowing might do the young plants grown from the fall sowing. Where the first and second crops are corn and the third winter wheat, the fourth should be timothy and clover for meadow. If clover be sown alone, it is preferable to use the mammoth variety and pasture it off until the 10th of June, earlier or later, according to the season, and then take a seed crop in the fall. If the common red be used in connection with timothy, it will, in favorable seasons, give the opportunity to take a seed crop if that is desired, and will in ordinary seasons, furnish a good supply of excellent pasture.

Let us now take account of the advantages of this rotation. If we have taken but one crop of corn, we have plowed the ground but once in three years; if two crops, but twice in four years. It is, therefore, economical of labor, a very important consideration. The soil has been kept full of living roots during the entire period in which the preparation of plant food by the microbes has been going on in the soil, except during the month of April and the first two weeks of May. It should be remembered that there is no waste of plant food during the winter, north of latitude forty, and but little south for some distance, for the double reason that the work of the microbes is suspended at this season and the ground remains frozen, so that there is no waste of fertility from washing. Another advantage is, that with the exception of the wheat and clover seed, which are cash crops, the entire product of this rotation is capable of profitable use as stock feed, and hence all is returned to the land in the form of manure—less the stock sold and the manure wasted.   A rotation of this sort will improve land to any extent desired, as the gradual increase of the mineral elements through the gradual decay of the rocky matter in the soil will more than make up for that sold in the form of grain, seed, or live stock.

In sections of the country where the character of the soil, the location and the taste of the farmer combine to make potato growing for commercial purposes profitable, this crop may be substituted for corn in the second year of the course. The cultivation of the potato crop prepares in advance a seed bed for winter wheat almost as favorable as corn, and has the advantage of avoiding the growing of the same crop on the same field in successive years.

In sections of the country where winter wheat is not reasonably sure, and rye has been found profitable, whether for the grain, or grain and straw combined, or for the purpose of obtaining some fall and spring pasture where tame grasses have not yet been established, it may be desirable to substitute rye for wheat, and when substituted, the rotation otherwise has about all the advantages enumerated above. These four crops, corn, potatoes, wheat or rye, or any combination of them, with clover as the beginning and the transition crop in the course from grass to grain, will form a profitable rotation. In fact, this four-course rotation, with clover or some other legume as the main grass crop, whether alone, or in combination with timothy, is a favorite rotation, and the one usually followed in all countries in the temperate zone, having an ample rainfall, where good farming has come to stay.

This four-course rotation may be used with almost equal advantage in sections where neither winter wheat, winter rye, nor potatoes can be grown profitably on a large scale, by substituting spring wheat, oats, or barley as the harvesters of the stored fertility of the clover crop. We might remark incidentally that the profit being equal, barley should be the first choice, spring wheat second, and oats third. In harvesting this stored fertility of the clover we should always keep an eye on the best and easiest way to get back to clover as the starting point for a new rotation. The main objection to any of these three spring grains is that their growth is necessarily rapid and luxuriant. They shade the ground densely in ordinary seasons and thus enfeeble the young clover plants. In wet seasons they are apt to lodge and smother out, while in dry seasons they make such large demands on the moisture of the soil, having to make their crop in about one hundred days, that the young clovers are robbed by a grain which is under the necessity of taking all the moisture that it can get, or fail of its mission—that of reproducing its kind as certainly and abundantly as possible.

If oats be selected as a nurse crop for clover, we strongly urge the selection of an early variety, one that will mature directly after winter wheat, and in so doing avoid at least half the danger of losing a stand of clover from the hot suns of the middle and last half of July. After our experience this year, we will never sow late oats when we hope for a stand of clover and timothy.

Some farmers find a three-years' course sufficient to utilize the stored fertility of the clover, and more particularly when they first begin to use it and before their land is brought up to its natural condition of fertility. I might remark here, by the way, that the experience of all countries is, that farmers do not usually begin to study farming in either a scientific or practical way, until they have first squandered the stored fertility of the thousands of years that have intervened since the surface of the earth took its present form. In this respect they are much like the young man who has inherited a fortune which he never helped to make, and hence does not know its value. If not, he must first spend the bulk of it before he begins to under-

stand the first principles of getting on in
the world independently of outside help.
The great majority of lands, either in timber or prairie countries, are thus exhausted
of a large amount of their available fertility, and when the farmer, like the prod-
igal in the parable, "comes to himself," he
will often find it an advantage to use only
two years, instead of three, in harvesting
his clover fertility, and hence is best
served by a short, or three-years' course,
after he has first secured a stand of clover.
He can transform the four-years' course
into a three, by simply dropping out the
second crop of corn or potatoes, and going directly from corn or potatoes, the
first crop after clover, to winter wheat,
rye, or either of the spring grains above
mentioned, and then getting back to clover. On the other hand, where farms have
been brought up by the three- or four-
years' course to their normal condition
of fertility, and in the meantime the farmer has become a stockman as well, he can
readily change the four-years' course into

a five, by using clover and timothy to seed down, and in the fifth year take either a crop of timothy seed, in which there will be more or less clover seed, or a crop of clover in which there will be more or less timothy, or use it as a pasture. In this he will have no more plowing of the land than in the four-years' course, and can gradually by this method decrease his grain raising and increase his stock farming, thus supplying himself with an additional amount of manure with which to increase the fertility of land already rich.

Alfalfa, in sections where it is used as a substitute for clover, does not fit nearly so well in the rotation which is necessary to harvest its stored fertility. In the first place it is only on certain lands that it can be used as a substitute and hence cannot come into general use in those sections of the country which have not as yet been able to avail themselves of the benefits of clover. In the second place it does not do nearly so well with a nurse crop, and hence requires the exclusive use of the land one year. In the third place it does not become so well established the first year as does clover, and hence the rotation must be longer. Three or four years will be required to get the profit out of an alfalfa seeding, and when once a stand has been secured, it is so valuable that the farmer is not willing to plow it up until he has had the advantage of more of the same sort of good forage crops. Probably as good a rotation as any in alfalfa sections would be the first, second and third years alfalfa, the fourth potatoes, and the fifth, winter wheat; after which the land can be prepared for seeding to alfalfa the next year.

In sections too remote from the market to make potato growing profitable, and where the elevation is not too great to grow corn, this might take its place; and where the elevation is too great, perhaps the best thing would be to plow under in August or the first of September after the second or third crop of alfalfa has been removed, and grow two or three crops of winter wheat in succession.

CHAPTER XV.

CLOVERS IN THE PASTURE AND FEED LOT.

SOLOMON, that wise old fellow who knew about everything that was worth knowing in his day, including farming—"sidewalk farmer" as he was—was accustomed to remark, as he noticed the failures of men to use properly that which cost them time, labor and money: "The slothful man roasteth not that which he took in hunting." We have often thought of Solomon's remark as we noticed farmers feeding out their clover hay. They have bought, or rented, land, gone to all the cost of preparing the soil, purchasing the seed, securing the stand, making the hay, and sometimes even providing a good shed or barn in which to keep it in its best condition, and then thrown away much of their gain, not

so much by a wasteful manner of feeding
it out, as by an injudicious selection of the
class of stock to which they feed it.   No
farmer would select a binder with which
to cut his meadow, nor a mower to cut
his wheat, if it stood up at all.   The average farmer shows much wisdom in select-
ing the tools which will do the most and
best work with a given amount of labor;
but he often fails to realize that clover,
whether in the pasture or in the feed lot,
is but one among many tools, and that its
work is quite different from that of his
other feeding tools, such as timothy, corn
fodder, oats straw, or the feed grains, such
as rye, oats, or barley.   If some farmers
could get over their prejudice against
book farming and listen for a little while
to what scientific men are trying to tell
them about the balanced ration, and the
food requirements of different kinds of
stock, and would follow out their teachings
in a practical, sensible way, they would
get a great deal more value out of their
clover, both in the pasture and in the feed
lot.

No farmer would long employ a physician in the family who was ignorant of the effects of his medicines, or who did not know the relative strength and efficiency of each ingredient in the dose. He would not employ a painter who did not know how to mix his paints so as to produce any desired color, or shade of color. The growing and feeding of animals for the market, is the main work of the advanced farmer. The various food stuffs on his farm are the raw materials, and it is altogether as important for him to know the composition of each, and the best method of mixing them to produce a definite result, as to know what kind of tools to select for a certain work, or for the physician to know the strength and effect of his medicines, or the painter to know the colors and the proper method of blending or mixing his paints.

In farming we begin the preparation of the seed bed with the plow, we finish it with the harrow; the physician breaks up the fever with one medicine, he completes the cure with another; the painter primes with one paint, he finishes with another. In handling live stock for profit, we first grow, then finish. The food for growth is mainly of one character, and for finishing, mainly of another. Profitable growth is made, always and everywhere, on foods consisting largely of flesh-formers, which the scientists call albumen, protein, and nitrogen, by which they mean the various compounds of nitrogen; while the finishing is done with foods composed largely of heat-makers and fat-formers, called carbohydrates. All foods carry carbohydrates as fuel power. As compared with the albuminoids, they vary, considering only the dry matter, from about four to one, to thirty to one. As every growing animal requires about five to one for health, we call all foods that have about the quantity the animal requires, or less, albuminoids; and those that contain much more fuel power than the animal requires, carbohydrates. The wise farmer, therefore, feeds albuminoids, and finishes off with foods rich in carbohydrates and in proportion to the requirements of the animal. Pregnant animals, milk cows and horses hard at work, require about the same sort of food as growing stock, and for very plain and obvious reasons. The horse hard at work is exercising his muscle and necessarily wasting it, and that waste must be repaired with muscle-making food, or albuminoids; hence, the intelligent farmer prefers oats as horse feed in the summer, and adds corn in winter to keep up the animal heat. The milk cow is furnishing a product rich in muscle-making material, hence needs muscle-making food; and the more milk she gives, the richer the food should be in albuminoids, or muscle-makers. The pregnant animal is developing the fœtus, composed of bone, gristle and water, and hence, needs a food well supplied with muscle-making, as well as bone-forming material.

Let us now apply these simple and obvious principles to feeding clover: first, in pasture. Clover in the early stages of its growth, is one of the very richest feeds, known to the farmer, the dry matter alone being considered. When in full bloom it has one of albuminoids to less than four of carbohydrates, and still less in the period preceding. It is then almost half as rich in albuminoids, the dry matter of each alone considered, as oil meal. As it matures it becomes more largely carbohydrate in its character, but still the richest of all growing plants in muscle-formers, hence its great value as a pasture for growing pigs—doubly valuable on Western farms because it prevents the incalculable injury that would otherwise be done by the "all corn" ration that constitutes the food of the pigs on so many farms of the West. Where steers under two years old are being finished and are expected to grow in flesh or muscle, as well as take on fat, no ration will accomplish the purpose so well as a pasture in which the clovers largely predominate in connection with dry or soaked corn and water.

It is customary in the fall of the year

for farmers to keep their cattle out of the stalk fields and on pastures, largely clover, until the snow covers the ground, and then to turn them into the corn fields.   There is usually more or less corn left from the husking which measurably decreases the waste of feed, otherwise inevitable, growing out of the fact that corn stalks have a ratio of one, to anywhere between twenty-five and thirty, depending on the exposure of the stalks to the weather.   The growth of young cattle on this kind of feed will be limited to the amount of flesh-formers contained therein, and the reason why young cattle shrink on corn stalks after the corn has been exhausted, is because they are compelled to eat and digest an enormous quantity of the stuff in order to utilize the small proportion of flesh-formers it contains.   Why not turn into the cornfields as soon as possible and allow the cattle to have the range, part of the day, of the clover pasture?   In this way they would utilize fully the clover, and at the same time give double value to

the food supplied by the corn stalks. They
would at least approximate in some degree
to the requirements of the cattle, to say
nothing of the greatly lessened danger of
impaction, the result of the vast amount
of super dry matter that they are compelled to consume in order to meet the
wants of the system.

A similar waste is constantly going on
in the feed lots on most farms. Farmers
usually keep one or two teams up in the
winter to do the running of the farm and
the chores. These horses have no more
exercise than is necessary for health. To
feed them clover hay is a waste, and especially so if they are fed oats as a grain
feed. All that horses need is enough of
muscle-formers to repair the waste of light
work, and carbohydrates to keep up the
animal heat. A moderate feed of oats
and corn, or oats straw and corn fodder,
is all that they require to keep them in
good condition. A farmer has a flock of
breeding ewes. They should be fed, not
with the idea of storing away fat, but of

providing for the growth of the fœtus and the wool, both of which require an albuminous ration. That is one place to use the clover hay. Clover hay alone, or clover and corn fodder, or sheaf oats and corn fodder, or better still, these alternating day by day, or in alternate feeds, is all that they require; and the less corn that is fed to them, the better for the lambs and the wool and the health of the sheep.

Another place to use the clover hay to very great advantage, is with the dairy cows. They are usually pregnant, large demands are made on the system for milk, and as they cannot make bricks without straw are the preferred class of stock, where there are no sheep on the farm to utilize the clover hay to the best advantage.

Except as a change of diet, always grateful to the animal, we would not give clover hay to mature steers on a full feed of grain, while it may be fed to advantage to yearlings which it is intended to finish for the market, for the reason above given, that these are expected to make a gain in flesh as well as in fat; and there is no form in which flesh-making, or muscle-making, elements can be given so cheaply as in the form of clover hay. Horses over two years old, if allowed to run in the blue grass pasture, even if covered with snow, with a hay stack, shelter, and plenty of salt and water, will get along well enough during the winter season; but the weanlings and yearlings should have a chance, if possible, at good clover hay. In short, the younger the animal, the stronger the claim it should have on the clover hay stored on the farm.

I am quite well aware that it is not always practical on the ordinary farm to carry out the suggestions above made. It is not always possible, nor, indeed, often possible, on the average farm, to so divide up the live stock as to give every one the portion best adapted to its wants, and the owner must do, as he is compelled to do in so many other things, the best he can. It is, however, important to know what is the theoretical best, and make it the practical best to as great an extent as possible. Where he is carrying mature stock through on the cheapest basis, he can readily find cheaper foods on the farm than he himself can furnish in the shape of clover hay. He should keep this one fact distinctly in mind, that clover hay is the only forage crop grown on the farm that is in itself anything like a balanced ration for growing stock, and that all other fodders, to which may be added corn, contain an excess of carbohydrates and need to be balanced with some muscle-making food in order to use them to the best advantage; and while clover hay will not balance up scientifically any of the straws, millet or corn fodder, it will, if fed in connection with these foods, render them almost doubly valuable, to say nothing of the food value of the clover itself.

In the above, I have been advising that which every observant farmer knows to be true in his own experience, and hence have not been adding anything to the sum of his knowledge. I have merely stated facts of which he is advised already, and needs only to be reminded.

CHAPTER XVI.

SUBSTITUTES FOR CLOVER.

THE farmer who has thoroughly mastered the art and science of clover growing in the Northern states, does not usually care to own land where clover does not do well. He has seen not only farms, but whole sections of country worn out by continuous cultivation. He knows by experience that the first of the great elements of fertility to be exhausted is the nitrogen, and if he cannot restore this element by clover, or some other leguminous crop, he must resort to commercial fertilizers containing nitrogen. If he cannot draw on the winds of heaven he must draw upon his pocketbook. He is not afraid to buy a so-called worn-out farm where he knows clover will grow, but he wisely declines unless he can grow either this great fertilizer and forage crop, or employ a substitute therefor.

The area on which clover does well is, after all, limited: on the west by a region of scant rainfall; in large sections of the South by extreme heat, as well as soils deficient in lime; and on the north by an extreme winter temperature. There are also sections in which the common clovers did well for a time, but will not now grow except in a long rotation. In many, in fact in most, sections of Europe, the land refuses to grow clover, except once in a seven or eight years' course. It is evident, therefore, that invaluable as clover is to a large section of the United States, there are very large areas on both continents for which substitutes must be provided.

I have written in vain if the reader does not clearly understand that one great value of clover lies in its ability to draw on the atmosphere for the nitrogen, with which it restores the wasted fertility of the soil, and also the muscle-making elements of animal food which render it so valuable in the pasture and barn. It thus becomes the handmaid and helper of grains and other grasses which are dependent for their nitrogen on the soil alone. It follows, therefore, that any substitute for clover must have the same power of using atmospheric nitrogen, and, therefore, must belong to the family of legumes, the only family, so far as known, that is in any way independent of the soil for its supply of nitrogen. No member of this family, however, possesses all the good qualities of the two larger varieties of clover, and hence the regions which grow these luxuriantly will always be among the most highly favored portions of the earth.

The two plants that come nearest taking the place of the red and mammoth clovers, are the crimson clover and alfalfa. The first is an annual, sown in August or September, and harvested in May or June. It has then fulfilled its mission. Crimson clover has been widely and persistently advertised as a valuable crop in the Middle and Northwestern states. It does not, however, suit either the climate or the agriculture of these sections, and I do not recommend it north of latitude forty, nor west of the Alleghany Mountains. It thrives, however, on the light soils of the Atlantic coast as far north as Delaware and New Jersey, and in this section is the sheet anchor of the "trucker," the market gardner, and the small farmer.

Of alfalfa I have spoken at length in Chapter VIII. While equal, if not superior to the larger clovers as a meadow grass, it is not nearly so valuable as pasture. Its cultivation is limited to lands capable of irrigation, or to lands with a porous subsoil in which it can send its roots down to permanent moisture, whether that be ten or thirty feet.

In many sections of the South, and in the semi-arid portions of the Western states, the sweet clover (melilotus alba) and bokara clover, take the place, to some extent, of the common clovers. In clover countries this plant is regarded as a weed, growing freely wherever sown by chance, along roadsides, or on rough waste lands, and valuable only as bee pasture. Stock do not relish it, and in towns where cattle have free range, it is seldom eaten when other grasses are abundant. When, however other grasses fail, it is found to have very considerable feeding value, and as a fertilizer, it is doubtful if it is exceeded, or even equaled by any of the clovers. It, therefore, can be used as a substitute in the sections already mentioned.

In latitude forty, and south to the Gulf, the soja or soy bean can be used to a certain extent as a substitute for the clovers, both as a fertilizer and forage plant. It can not, however, be used as a pasture, and is a grain, rather than a forage crop, but can be used as a forage crop in the same way that we use corn when cut for fodder. The Southern states have not yet learned the value of the soy bean.

In the more southern sections where the common clovers fail on account of the excessive heat, or the lack of the necessary elements in the soil, or where neither al-

falfa nor crimson clover thrive, perhaps
the best of all known substitutes for the
larger clovers is the cow pea. There are
varieties of this valuable plant adapted to
almost any variety of soil and climate as
far north as latitude forty-two. It can be
sown early or late, and in the extreme
South, as late as the last of July as the
second crop of the year. It is especially
valuable as a fertilizer in sections where
owing to the heat, decomposition is very
rapid and the rainfall so excessive that the
nitrates are washed out of the soil as fast
as formed. So long as the atmosphere is
four-fifths nitrogen, and the cow pea has
tubercles on its roots, there is no need of
the Southern farmer exhausting the fertil
ity of land, naturally rich in the mineral
elements. If he will but sow cow peas in
his corn, or between crops of cotton and
either pasture, mow, or plow under the
crop, he will have an unfailing source of
nitrogen.

The cow pea can be used to advantage
in the latitudes of southern Missouri, Kan

sas, and south wherever clover does not flourish. Sown on fallow ground in any section, it will prove a valuable substitute for clover both as a fertilizer and forage crop.

Neither has a kind Providence left any country without a substitute for white clover, so valuable in the pasture. Its place is taken in the South by the Japan clover, so-called (lespedeza striata). This was introduced by accident into the South Atlantic states about fifty years ago, and during that time has spread over almost the entire Southern country. Like nearly all substitutes for clover in a climate of great and long continued summer heat, it is an annual, beginning to ripen its seeds in August and continuing until killed by frost. It does not, except in the richest bottom lands, produce sufficient forage to justify cutting it for a hay crop, but it is through all the South a good Samaritan, providing its own charges, sowing itself wherever there is an abandoned field, and thus binding up the broken-hearted land. Like the clovers and all the legumes, it has the power of storing the soil with nitrogen, and is thus a boon to the Southern farmer of which he is only beginning to appreciate the value.

Even in the pine forests of Texas and Arkansas, where nature seems to frown at any effort to grow crops beyond watermelons and sweet potatoes, we have found growing, wherever there was a chance of sunlight, a small vining clover with a pod like a pea, containing four seeds, known as the Carolina clover, and which is certainly worthy of cultivation in those sections, and on the richer lands as well, as a a pasture grass. Unlike the Japan clover, this is said to be a perennial, hence doubly valuable.

For California with its two seasons—its wet winter and rainless summer—Providence, ever thoughtful of the herds and flocks, has provided the bur clover (medicago denticulata), a relative of alfalfa and a plant of great economic value, whether as a natural fertilizer or pasture grass. It grows during the rainy season, produces an abundance of seed in the form of burs, which in the dry season take the place of grain in the feeding of live stock. I have seen sheep by the thousand feeding and apparently thriving on the seeds of the bur clover in fields seemingly as bare of verdure as the well-trodden highway. This clover reaches eastward into western Texas, and a closely related variety (medicago maculata) may be found on the sandy plains of western Nebraska.

Without going into the subject exhaustively, it will be readily seen that in sowing these clovers and clover-like plants over all portions of North America, capable of a systematic agriculture or profitable pasturage, the Lord of the herds and flocks, as well as of men, had in mind plans of vast benevolence. He has provided in these plants flesh- and muscle-formers for the flocks and herds in winter as well as summer; ordained, also, that man should not be without the means of restoring fertility to the soil after it had been **apparently** exhausted by his improvidence **and greed.** If to the northern and central **Mississippi** Valley states He has given **the best** of the clovers and legumes, it **was because** these states were intended to **be the granary** of the continent—the source **of** supplying bread and meats to the **hungry** nations of the Old World. He did **not intend** that any portion of this continent **should** be doomed to sterility and **barrenness** through the folly of man, but **has provided** in the clover and clover-like **plants a** means of restoring fertility to the **land** of every farmer and stock-grower **who is** willing to work with Him in carrying out His vast schemes of benevolence toward all **His creatures.**

www.ingramcontent.com/pod-product-compliance
Lightning Source LLC
Chambersburg PA
CBHW030823020726
47499CB00006B/2050